THE
GIRL IN THE BROKEN MIRROR

SAVITA KALHAN

THE GIRL IN THE BROKEN MIRROR

troika

Published by TROIKA

First published in the UK in 2018

Troika Books Ltd

Well House, Green Lane, Ardleigh CO7 7PD, UK

www.troikabooks.com

A CIP catalogue record for this book is available
from the British Library

ISBN 978-1- 909991-63-7

2 3 4 5 6 7 8 9 10

Printed in Poland

For Hish, Jad and Taghreed,
as always.

'There are many stories
Which are not on paper,
They're written in the
bodies and minds of women.'
Amrita Pritam

PROLOGUE

The sunlight blazed obscenely through her windows, blinding, dazzling. It stretched out its long, warm fingers towards her, but Jay did not let them touch her. She reached for the alarm clock and turned it off. The alarm had been going for ages and the clock said nine fifteen. She hadn't heard it ringing before because of the incessant buzzing in her ears. The buzzing hadn't stopped all night. Only now did it fade away a little and allow her to hear.

She hadn't closed her eyes after . . . after *he* had gone. She had lain amid the soiled sheets, staring into empty space, all night. There were no tears. There was nothing inside her but a huge empty well. She couldn't, wouldn't, close her eyes again. *His* face was in there, and if she closed her eyes she would see it.

A quiet tapping on her door startled her, but Jay did not respond. She waited, listening, and heard her mother's soft voice. It found a way through the faint buzz that was still in Jay's ears and made her aware of the hollow inside her. She stuffed her hand in her mouth and moaned silently. There were still no tears.

'Jaya, *beti*, are you sleeping?' Her mum's voice dropped to a whisper – 'It's all right. Don't get up yet – it is very early. I'm going out for a little while, to the *mandir*' – and then her footsteps moved away from the door, fading until Jay couldn't hear them any more.

She wanted to call her back.

She wanted her mother to come back and hold her and rock her and say, 'Everything will be all right. Don't worry. I'm here, Jaya.' Her mother would never call her *beti*, her darling daughter, again. How could she, after what had happened?

It was too late to call her back. Her mum had gone to the temple to pray. And emptiness filled the space she had left behind.

The clock ticked loudly, punctuating every moment of silence as it approached ten o'clock. Time was moving on, leaving Jay stranded behind. Ten o'clock came and went. She heard the muffled vibration of her phone. She knew who it was. Matt. Her best friend, her soulmate and, recently, much more. But that would be history now.

Every few minutes, the phone vibrated again and again, but she could not answer his calls. She could not speak. The phone stopped ringing eventually. Complete silence descended once more.

Another knock on the door. A loud rapping this time.

'Jay? It's Ash. Jay?' He knocked insistently and Jay thought for a minute that he might just open the door and barge in. She held her breath. She'd forgotten that he'd offered to fit a bolt to her door. He'd thought he'd saved her, and then he'd gone up to bed. He didn't know. No one knew about what had happened later.

After knocking on the door a few more times, he went away too. She didn't call him back either. The bolt was useless now. Worthless.

Only when it got to midday did her brain begin to hum sluggishly, and she started to think – not about what had happened, because her brain would shut down even at the briefest image of it. But she thought about her mum, and how she did not want her mum to see her like this. She usually got back from the *mandir* around two o'clock.

Jay had to do something. She had to get up. She had to wash, clean herself up. Make herself look respectable for her mother. Make herself look as though nothing had happened to her. That was what she had to do.

And beyond that, her mind was a blank.

She pushed back the bedcovers and swung her legs out of bed, and fell back as the pain hit her. Everything hurt. Moving more slowly, she gingerly raised herself off the bed. Her legs shook so hard she had to hold on to the bedside table for support. She leaned heavily on it until the dizziness passed, her legs still trembling. Sobs tore through her clenched teeth as she forced herself to stand.

She did not want to look down, but her eyes went that way anyway. They made her look. They made her stare. They made her see the things she already knew were there. The things she did not want to see.

The bruises, the dried blood and the sticky stuff on her legs. She moaned and then retched violently several times. There was enough to clean up without having to mop up sick too.

She hobbled across the narrow space to the chest of drawers, picking her bathrobe up on the way. She fumbled with the knot, which her stiff fingers refused to tie, and caught sight of the four half-moon indentations etched deeply into each of her palms. As she stared at the perfect marks, her brain shut down once more. The room blurred, and she slumped against the chest of drawers and slid down to the ground. She curled up, hugging her knees to her chest, gently rocking herself. Jay did not know how long she stayed like that.

She had to get up before the black void returned.

She dragged herself up and gathered a pile of clean clothes. She paused at the door, making sure there was no one there, before stumbling across to the bathroom, weaving through the debris strewn across the wooden floor of the gym next to her basement room, and holding her breath against the sickening stench of stale alcohol. She stepped inside the bathroom and locked the door.

Jay dropped her clothes on the floor and switched the temperature gauge in the shower to its hottest setting. Soon the room was enveloped in steam. She removed her bathrobe and the remains of her pyjamas, and stepped under the scalding water.

It burned her, but it didn't take away the other pain. And emptying a bottle of shower gel didn't make her feel any cleaner.

She tipped the contents of almost a whole bottle of Dettol on to her body, and put the rest on to a sponge and scoured her skin with it.

Scoured each and every part of her body that hurt.

She cried through all of it, not realizing she was crying until she'd stepped out of the shower and was standing in front of the mirror over the sink. She wiped the steam away with one hand, the other steadying her on the sink so she did not fall, and she caught sight of her face. It was red raw from the hot water. Her right eye was bulging, the bruising livid shades of purple and black. Her lip was swollen and cut. Her eyes were empty.

This was not Jay. This was someone else.

As she stared at the stranger in the mirror, her tears ran dry and the numbness returned. Jay put on her clothes and stumbled back to her room. And then she heard the murmur of voices from the garden.

They were out there, the whole family, having lunch in the sunshine. She heard Aunty Vimala's voice. Then another voice spoke.

She covered her ears, but the muffled voices still made themselves heard. She didn't want to hear them. She did not want to hear *his* voice. She couldn't stay here. She had to get away. She had to leave.

Jay bundled a few clothes into a rucksack and found a baseball cap to hide beneath, but she had too much hair and it was dripping wet. She stood in front of her pink-heart mirror and tried dragging the hairbrush through it. Large droplets of water sprayed the air. There were too many knots and no time. The rise and fall of the voices in the garden felt too close; she had to get away from them. She tugged the hairbrush harder, but her frustration made the long tangled mess worse and she began to cry. And then the brush was flying out of her hands straight at the mirror, hitting it with a crack. The mirror split in two, splintering the reflection of her face, a face she didn't want to look at anyway because it was repulsive and grotesque.

The girl in the broken mirror was not Jay.

She twisted her hair back into a ponytail and tied it at the base of her neck with a scrunchy. In a drawer she found a sharp pair of scissors. With it all still tied up it was easy to hack it off.

Snip, snip, snip, and it was gone. No more tangles.

She tossed the ponytail in the bin and pulled what was left of her hair around her face, obscuring her ugly face, with its hideous black eye, and then covered it up with the peak of the cap pulled low.

The voices were still in the garden. She had to hurry. There wasn't much to tidy up – it wasn't much of a room, this place she'd tried to call home. She picked up the two ends of the duvet and gave it a shake, holding it low in front of her so she wouldn't inadvertently catch a glimpse of the sheet, before throwing it back on the bed and smoothing it down.

She didn't need to see the sheet; she knew what was on it, and there was no need for anyone else to see it either.

At the doorway, she hesitated. Her possessions, her precious, paltry belongings saved first from the bailiffs after her dad had died, then saved from the poky flat she and her mum couldn't afford, were now to be abandoned here. She didn't need them. There was nothing she wanted except her books, and those she could not carry.

She approached the top of the basement stairs with her heart in her mouth, her greatest fear that someone might see her. But the hallway was deserted. She let herself out of the house and gently clicked the front door shut behind her, and began walking down the street.

She walked and she walked, letting her unsteady feet lead her on, not knowing where they were taking her, and not caring. They could take her anywhere. Anywhere was better than here.

Tears marched unsteadily down her face, keeping time with her faltering pace. Houses passed by in a blur of bricks and windows, streets came and went, the rush of passing cars echoed in her ears, and only the loud blaring of car horns reminded her that she had stepped off the pavement and into the road. She walked for hours. She had no idea what time it was and never thought to look at her watch. She had to keep walking until she could think properly, until she knew where she was going, until she knew what she was going to do.

She could have gone to Ash. Sweet, shy Ash, her ally in the house. But what would he tell her to do? Family was family, blood thicker than water. She didn't really count as family, but *he* did.

She didn't know whether she could tell anyone

what had happened, say the words that needed to be said. She could barely think them.

A part of her mind told her that there were people she could go to who would take him away. Arrest him. That he was a criminal. But until she could say the word for what had happened to her – that terrible, vile, shameful word – she couldn't even begin to think about that. All she could do was to carry on walking, and get as far away as possible from No.42 Primrose Avenue.

She should have gone to Matt. No, no, no – she could never do that. Never. He would not want her now. No one would want her. Even her mother would not be able to look at her without feeling shame. There would never be a place Jay could hide that shame, bury it deep enough; she would never be free of it. It would taint her like a livid scar until the day she died.

Jay stumbled, her legs suddenly refusing to obey her. She put her hand out to break her fall, and found the brick wall of someone's front garden. She sank down on it for a moment, arms clutched tightly around herself, rocking backwards and forwards, as though rocking would ease the pain.

It took her a while to realize that she was being watched. In the driveway, a young couple were unloading shopping bags from the boot of their car. They were watching her and talking in whispers. It was the whispers that penetrated the fog around her.

What were they saying? Were they wondering who this girl was and how she had got into this state?

How had she, Jayalakshmi Sharma, ended up here, like this, right now?

PART ONE

Before.
Several months earlier . . .

CHAPTER 1

Glancing up at the rapidly darkening sky, the heavy clouds threatening to burst at the seams and drench anything foolish enough to lie in their path, Jay broke into a run. She should have come straight home after school instead of hanging out at the cafe with Matt and Chloe, but the thought of the long solitary evening ahead hadn't exactly made her want to hurry back to the empty flat. With a frenzied burst of energy, she dashed past the parade of shops and reached her front door. As she slotted her key in the lock, a drop of rain licked her face and then another trickled down her neck. She pushed the door shut behind her as the thunderous downpour let loose with a vengeance.

She flicked the light switch on and headed up the stairs, and then headed straight back down, with a groan, as she realized she hadn't collected her box of veg from the grocer's shop downstairs. Mr Hope gave her the veg that was just past its best, for pennies – only it never looked past its best to her. He'd given her a weekend job too, helping out in the shop, and he'd insisted on paying her a fair wage. She gave most of it to her mum, and if it was a good week, Mum gave her some of it back.

'Goodnight, Mr Hope,' she called as she left the grocer's.

'Mind you don't get too wet, love.'

The rain was falling in vertical sheets by the time Jay ran across the front of the shop and back through her front door. She pushed the door shut with her heel, balancing the box in one hand while she scooped up her school bag with the other, and went up to the flat. The first thing she always did when she came in was switch on some lights and the radio. It made the flat feel more alive, more like Matt's house or Chloe's. Their mums were usually at home when they got in.

No one was home when Jay got in. As an only child she was used to not having siblings around, and over the last couple of years, she'd had to get used to her mum not being around much either. But that wasn't out of choice; that was out of necessity. And as for her dad – well, he'd died three years ago, and shortly after that they'd found out they were broke. At eleven and a half years old, Jay had not been able to get her head round it at all, but at fourteen she was a very different person.

No one could call her a 'rich bitch' now, which was what some of the other kids called her when she'd first started at Kingswell Secondary halfway through Year Seven, and they'd found out what kind of school she used to go to. The most hurtful insult had been: 'spoiled little daddy's brat'. To be fair, it was only one particular clique, led by the infamous Ms – Marissa and May – who indulged in name-calling. And that was before they found out where she lived, and that her dad was dead. Then they called her 'Little Orphan Annie'. Jay hid inside her shell, ignoring them. She turned twelve and no one at her new school even knew it was her birthday. After a while they pretty much left her alone – at least, they had until it was obvious she and Matt were best mates.

She took off her school uniform and put on a tracksuit and jumper, shivering as the cold brought goosebumps to her skin. They were trying to be more careful after the last gas bill, but it was so cold Jay could see her breath swirling in little puffs. She managed to resist for about fifteen minutes, but ended up switching the heating on to stop icicles forming on the ceiling, and then she jumped up and down and clapped her hands to get some feeling back in them while she waited for the kettle to boil.

Her hands cupped round a steaming mug of hot chocolate, Jay headed to her bedroom to make a start on her English homework.

She chewed the end of her pen, staring up at the mottled-brown stained ceiling, at the damp patch in the corner that had come right through the pink paint she'd only reapplied last week, and back down at the blank page of her exercise book.

She had a story in her head, and it was perfect for her English homework.

'For your creative writing exercise, I want you to write a fairy tale,' Mrs Hargreaves had said. 'Start it with "Once upon a time" and end it with . . . "and they lived happily ever after". Include tragedy and conflict, princes and princesses if you want, rags to riches, good and evil, hopes and dreams, et cetera. All the things we've discussed,' she concluded, with a wave of her hand.

The only problem with Jay's story idea was the ending. A happy ending would be a real struggle to write. Did they even exist in real life? Jay and her mum had thought they were living the happily ever after bit, but then it all went horribly wrong. And the way life was panning out, Jay wasn't sure she would ever reach it.

She plugged in her earphones and searched for Nina

Simone on her iPod. It was her dad's fault she was into a jazz singer none of her friends had ever heard of. He used to play her all the time. His dream had been to go and see her perform live, but he hadn't managed to before she died. Now he was dead too.

If looking at her dismal surroundings hadn't given her any inspiration for the tragic tale she was about to embark on, thinking about her dad did the trick. Jay hit play and as 'I Wish I Knew How it Would Feel to Be Free' poured into her ears, she began writing the story of how the beautiful Queen Neem and her young daughter, Princess Jala, had lost their beloved King Aravind in a skirmish with an invading band of marauders on the outskirts of their kingdom, and how, shortly afterwards, they lost their fortune to the king's wicked and unscrupulous advisor. Shunned by the royal courtiers and by the people who they had once thought to be loyal to them, the queen and princess found themselves alone and destitute in a filthy hovel far from their kingdom, scratching a meagre living, mired in poverty.

As she read back through what she'd written so far, Jay began to wonder if the parallels were too obvious. It wouldn't matter unless Mrs Hargreaves intended to have some of the stories read aloud. Then it would matter big time. Perhaps she should change the names: Princess Jala had to become Princess Nala, and Queen

Neem could become Queen Alima, she decided. The rest of the piece could stay as it was, because only Matt and Chloe knew the whole story of her sad little life.

An hour into her homework, and satisfied with the pages she'd written, Jay took a break to cook dinner, so it would be ready for when Mum got home from her cleaning job. She rummaged through the veg box and decided on a potato and cauliflower curry with some tarka dhal. Marta would come by at seven o'clock, to pick Mum up for the teacher-training course they were both doing at evening college. Tuesdays were always a mad rush for Jay's mum. Tuesdays and Thursdays and Saturdays. Her mum was almost always exhausted. She held down two jobs while also doing her part-time course, which would hopefully lead to a teaching job and a ticket out of their dilapidated flat above the grocer's shop. That would be the 'and they lived happily ever after' part, Jay hoped.

She had her own plan, which was just as frustratingly long-term. She had to do brilliantly in her GCSEs and even more brilliantly in her A Levels, so she could get a scholarship to university and then get a brilliant job. Jay hacked the coriander leaves to within an inch of their lives, threw them in the pot and slammed on the lid. The back-up plan was good – as long she didn't stop and think about it for too long. She would have loved to have been like the rest of her class and not have to think any further than what film to go and see at the cinema.

Dinner was almost ready. She was tempted to go out and buy some naans to go with it, but Mum would tell her off for wasting money when there was a whole sack of chapatti flour sitting in the cupboard. She took two cupfuls, tipped them into a bowl and added water, to knead it into a soft, pliable dough.

It was a shame Matt couldn't come round tonight. This was his favourite meal. Since he'd started spending more and more time at the flat with her, the long, lonely evenings without Mum had become a thing of the past. He shared Jay's plan to get out of Kingsbury. They wanted to end up at the same uni, so they studied together most nights – but whereas she got labelled a swot, no one would ever call Matt anything other than cool.

Jay switched all the hobs off and went back to her room. She picked up the story where she had left off, but found it hard to get back into it. Her thoughts kept drifting back to Matt, and back to all the distracting things that had recently started happening.

They usually walked down the road with their arms linked, the way best friends do, but last week he'd taken her hand, and this week he'd kissed her – it was only a peck on the cheek, but for Jay there was nothing 'only' about it. She had felt her insides tingle in a way she'd never experienced before. Since then she'd begun to see him differently too, and she could understand why he was the boy every girl in Year Ten wanted to go out with. He was tall, athletic, dark-haired and brown-eyed, with a face chiselled to perfection by the gods. No wonder the two Ms hated her!

The bonus with Matt was that he was a laugh, and clever, and kind too . . . Jay groaned at herself. She was beginning to sound like one of the girls in his massive fan club. She had to stop thinking about him, and get back to the essay.

Maybe Princess Nala should meet a tall, dark prince, who . . .

The front door slammed.

'Jaya? Are you home?' her mum called.

'I'm in here,' Jay called back, although she didn't know why she bothered raising her voice in their tiny little flat, which was so small that her mum slept on a pull-out settee in the living room.

Jay's mum appeared in the doorway. 'Have you eaten?' she asked, pulling off her cleaning apron and folding it up ready for Thursday.

'No, I waited for you. I've cooked though.'

Her mum smiled gratefully. 'You are such a good girl, Jaya.'

Oh God, if she only knew the truth, Jaya thought. Sure, she was good about helping out round the flat

– doing the chores and cooking, which she had to learn very quickly because she was fed up of eating sandwiches every night. She worked at the grocer's shop downstairs most weekends too. But the bad part, the part that mattered even more to her traditional Indian mum, was the fact that no matter how hard Jay tried, she couldn't make herself more Indian.

It had been better when her dad was still alive. Although he was born and bred in the Punjab, in Northern India, he was her ally against all things Indian – having decided, from the moment he'd stepped off the plane at Heathrow, to totally immerse himself in the way of life here.

And then there was Matt, and the weird feelings she suddenly had for him too.

'Go and get changed and I'll warm the food up and make some rotis,' Jay said, closing her exercise book.

Her mother hesitated for a moment. 'There is something we must talk about, but it will wait until we are sitting down. Give me ten minutes.'

There was a funny look in her mum's eyes and for a moment Jay wondered if she had seen her and Matt holding hands.

'We have been here for almost three years, Jay,' her mum began tentatively, at dinner. She tucked a stray wisp of hair back in the bun at the nape of her neck.

Jay remembered her mum had glossy black hair then, still cut in a trendy bob. Now it was liberally sprinkled with shiny silver strands and tied up in an old-woman bun. She'd stopped bothering with her contact lenses and wore glasses instead. No one would think she was barely forty. Chloe, Jay's other best friend, had a stepdad, but Jay knew her mum would never remarry. Indian women like her mum never did.

That date was coming up, Jay suddenly realized. That's why her mum was acting all weird.

'Mum, it's OK. I'll go to the temple with you on the anniversary,' Jay said resignedly. 'And I'll try not to freak out.'

Three years had passed since her dad had wrapped his car round a tree for no apparent reason; it hadn't been snowing or foggy, or even raining. He had been killed instantly. What no one knew then was he had just found out that he had lost his business.

That first time she had gone to the temple with her mum after his death was a day that Jay had tried to forget. They had taken their shoes off in the entrance to the temple, her mum nudging her to cover her hair before going inside. They'd bowed their heads at the shrine and placed money in the offering tray, then sat down, cross-legged, on the white-sheeted floor.

That was when everything went wrong.

Sitting in silence, surrounded by the sweet smell

of incense and soft, murmured voices in prayer, Jay had looked down at her clasped hands, tears of anger prickling her eyes, trying to work out what she was doing there. What would praying do now? It wouldn't bring her dad back; it wouldn't send her back to her old school, St Montague's, which she had loved with a passion; it wouldn't give her back her old friends, her old care-free life. She used to get thirty pounds pocket money a week, and never thought that that was a lot of money for an eleven year old.

Now she did their weekly supermarket shop with less money than that.

Being in the temple, an environment that felt totally alien to her, had also brought back all the terrible memories she had worked hard to forget. They came crashing back with such violence that Jay had run out on to the street barefoot, tears streaming down her face. The empty, hollow space inside her threatened to suck her in. She had refused to go with her mum the following year. But she was sure she could do it for her mum without the histrionics or drama this time. She wasn't that overwrought little girl any more.

Her mum leaned across the table and squeezed Jay's hand.

'Thank you, Jaya. But there is something else . . .'

Her mum pulled away.

CHAPTER 2

Oh God, Jay thought, here we go.

A stab of panic sent her fork clattering on to the lino floor. Her mum must have guessed about Matt. She knew having a boy as a best friend was eventually going to cause problems between her and her mum. She should have paid more attention to the recent coolness in her mum's attitude towards him. She made a mental note to invite Chloe over a lot more, at least for a little while.

'We are going to move,' her mum finally declared.

Jay's face fell. 'What? Why? I can't, Mum. I'm not moving school again.'

'Don't worry,' her mum said quickly. 'You will continue at the same school, so you will not be losing your friends and having to begin again. I remember how upsetting it was for you when you had to leave St Montague's, Jaya.'

'Phew! So where is it then?' Jay asked, taking a sip of orange juice. 'Where are we going?' Her mother was suddenly unwilling to meet her eyes. She was pushing her food around with a piece of roti. Wherever they were moving to, it wasn't going to be good, Jay sensed. 'Mum?'

'It is in a lovely area, on the other side of the school. It will be so much safer for you, Jaya. I worry about you walking around in the dark here.'

Her mum's bright, cheerful tone only made Jay more anxious. 'This area's fine, Mum. Anyway, Matt always walks me back if it's late.' Damn! She shouldn't have mentioned Matt. Her mum was frowning now. 'And Chloe doesn't live too far from here,' she added. 'I've been walking home from school for the last few years, so why's it suddenly so unsafe now that I'm fourteen? Where are we going, Mum?'

Her mum set her fork down and looked up. Jay was both puzzled and perplexed by the pleading expression on her face. 'We are moving to Primrose Avenue.'

Jay almost choked on her juice.

'Your Vimala Aunty and Uncle Bal have kindly offered us rooms in their house, and it will be good for us, Jaya.'

'No! We can't move there, Mum,' Jay protested.

Horrified didn't even begin to describe how Jay felt about moving in with Aunty Vimala.

'We have to,' Neela replied. 'Mr Hope has been kind to us – he hasn't raised the rent in two years, he gave you a job, he gives us groceries . . . but he is retiring, Jaya.'

'So . . . he's selling the flat?'

'Yes, and the shop too. But even with the help he gave us, it was difficult to save any money. Your Uncle and Aunty will not ask us for any rent money, Jaya.'

'I'm still not moving there, Mum.'

'It has been decided,' Jay's mother said firmly.

'But this is the first I've heard about it! We haven't even talked about it.'

'It is my decision to make.'

Jay pushed her plate away angrily. She could not believe this was happening. 'Well, I'm not moving there!'

'Why do you have to be so stubborn? What do you have against them?'

'Nothing . . . Everything! Please, Mum. Don't make me go there.'

Her mum sighed wearily. 'I will not argue about this, Jaya. I have decided. We will move next weekend.'

'What's the hurry?'

'The flat is going on the market on Monday, and we cannot afford another place like this.' Her mum bit her lip. 'I am so sorry, Jaya, *beti*. It's for the best. We can save some money by living with your uncle and aunty.

They will not charge us any rent, and we only have to help out in the house. It will be for a short while, Jaya.'

Jay looked at the cold food on her plate. Tears stung her eyes, but before they could fall, she snatched up her plate and took it through to the kitchen, ignoring her mum's pleas to sit back down and finish her food.

'I'll finish it later,' she muttered, heading for her room.

Jay blasted out Adele's 'Rolling in the Deep' at top volume, wallowing in how unfair everything was.

She hadn't seen her uncle and aunt since her dad died, but she remembered Uncle Bal as a quiet, self-effacing man who had made a fortune in Indian ready meals before selling the business and retiring. He was a distant relative of her mum's. Despite his success, he wasn't given to airs or graces, unlike his wife, who had acquired so many airs and graces that she'd had to build several extensions on the house to accommodate them. She was a particular kind of Indian woman, one who had super-strict rules for girls and very different ones for boys, and the same went for her expectations of them. She would expect Jay to come home after school and put Indian clothes on. She'd expect her to help out with all the cooking and cleaning. She would not expect her to have lots of friends, and definitely none that were boys. She would expect Jay only to have

Indian friends, if she insisted on having friends at all.

That was a lot to expect of someone like Jay.

Jay thumped her pillow hard, and then thumped it a few more times for good measure. There had to be a way out – but if there was, Jay couldn't think of it.

Her dad had never been like that. He'd been determined to leave all that hypocrisy – the caste stuff, the rules and restrictions – behind him when he'd emigrated. Jay knew he'd felt belittled by her mum's parents. They'd never thought he was good enough, and his family had been considered way too 'out there'. There was an artist in his family, which they found shocking enough, and Jay's aunty even made Indian pop videos! Her dad was the most traditional of all his siblings: he'd gone to uni and got a Business and Economics degree. He'd always wanted to live in England. He'd never cared that he didn't have a son, either. He'd always told Jay that she was better than a million boys.

Her mum, on the other hand, obviously came from a far more conservative background, and although she had defied her parents by marrying someone against their wishes, it wasn't as though he was from a different caste or anything. She wasn't a real rebel. Not like Jay's dad.

Jay looked down at the cover of her exercise book and grimaced when she saw what she'd doodled.

Indianness

Low   Ridiculously High

| | | | |

Jay   Dad   Mum   Gandhi   Aunty Vimala

When Jay thought about it, Aunty Vimala's Indianness was probably even off the scale she'd drawn. It was the kind that clung with grim determination to a way of life that had long since disappeared. Times had moved on in India, but in Primrose Avenue, they'd ground to a halt, trapped in a time warp of India circa 1950.

That's what Jay would be trapped in.

Uncle Bal and Aunty Vimala had two boys – Ash, their younger son, who was two years older than Jay, and Deven, who was two or three years older than Ash – but she hadn't seen either of them since her dad's funeral. Ash was geeky and Deven was loud, that's all she remembered about them. Maybe, just maybe, they would protect her from Aunty Vimala's prying eyes, so she'd still have some kind of social life while she was forced to live in Primrose Avenue.

'You haven't heard a word I've said, have you?' Chloe said, waving her mascara brush in Jay's face. 'We're meeting up in Nando's and then we're going to the cinema. Is that OK for you?'

Jay glanced up at her friend. 'What? Sorry, Chlo. This weekend? I don't think I'll be able to make it.'

Chloe sighed and put her mascara away, after a quick check in her make-up mirror. 'What's up with you today, Jay?'

They were sitting on the wall outside the lunch room. The rain had gone, leaving the playground tarmac shimmering in the sunshine. The weather was supposed to be good at the weekend. Nando's and the cinema sounded good too.

Jay groaned aloud. 'What am I going to do, Chloe? I've only got one week of freedom left.'

Chloe's sky-blue eyes widened with surprise. 'You what?' she exclaimed. 'Explain,' she demanded.

In the playground, kids were milling around – some messing about with a football, the younger ones playing a complicated game of tag. School would be the only place where she'd have any freedom soon. It was a depressing thought. 'I'm moving. To Primrose Avenue. We'll be staying with some distant relatives of my mum's and it'll be like living in the Dark Ages,' Jay said despondently.

'What do you mean? Can't we still hang out?'

Jay shook her head. 'I won't be allowed out and my aunt won't like me having people over.'

'Are you seriously telling me that I can't come over to see you?'

'I don't know.' Jay kicked the wall angrily with her heel. 'But I'll know soon enough. We're moving next weekend.'

'Your aunt will love me. I'll switch on the charm. Just wait and see. Hey, Primrose Avenue? Isn't that near Matt? He'll be happy.' Chloe winked, an impish grin on her face. 'You'll be practically round the corner from him.'

If Chloe didn't understand, how was Matt going to get his head round it? 'Fat use that will be if he can't come over and I can't go out. Chloe, my aunt is . . . Well, she's mega traditional – at least as far as girls are concerned. I'm sure she thinks it's a waste of time for Indian girls to even bother with school. In any spare time I have she'll be making me cook and clean the house. And if I try to go out, she'll probably lock me up in my room!'

Chloe tossed her head back, making her long blond hair cascade down her back, and laughed. 'Don't be silly. She'll soon realize you're not a *proper* Indian girl, Jay!'

'Kind of wish I was though,' Jay said quietly. 'It would make this so much easier.' Her lips quivered and tears threatened to make an unwelcome appearance. She'd argued with her mum about it all night, but her mum refused to budge. 'I'm not bad. I'm just not . . . Indian enough to live with them. Not their kind of Indian.'

Jay almost wished that Chloe was Indian, then she might have understood. But she wasn't, and Jay didn't have any close Indian friends. The Indians they had known when she was younger, when her dad was still alive, had mostly been wealthy business friends whose lifestyles weren't bound by traditions and customs. After her dad died, they'd disappeared. Her mum said she had no time to stay in touch with them, which was true, but Jay thought it was because they didn't have any time for people who weren't rich like them.

Chloe linked her arm through Jay's. 'Cheer up, Jay. Your aunty might have changed for all you know. She might be really nice now.'

'You wanna bet? She's not even my real aunty, just a distant relative. And I hate the fact that Mum went begging to her for help. She's probably loving getting one up on us. Sorry, Chloe. Sounds like I'm being really ungrateful, doesn't it?'

'Look, you can sneak over to mine whenever you need to escape. We'll have lots of sleepovers. Mum won't mind, and I know your mum likes me.'

'Thanks, Chloe.' But Jay had a feeling that her mum wasn't going to allow anything that Aunty Vimala didn't approve of. 'I haven't told Matt yet, so don't say a word.'

'Say a word about what?' Matt said, throwing an arm over Jay's shoulder, trying to plant a kiss on her cheek.

'Matt!' She pushed him away, frowning.

'Yeah, control yourself, Gardener! I don't appreciate being made a gooseberry,' Chloe huffed.

Jay felt a blush rising on her cheeks. 'Don't be silly! Where's Alex anyway?' Alex was Chloe's long-standing boyfriend, but recently Chloe never seemed to want to hang out with him at school.

'Football practice, or something equally boring,' Chloe said dismissively.

Matt linked arms with both of them. 'Is that better?' he asked, looking from Jay to Chloe. 'Anyone going to tell me what's going on?'

The bell for afternoon registration rang, saving Jay from having to tell him just then. 'Can you come back to the flat with me after school?' she asked.

'Yeah, of course.'

She could tell he knew something was up from the look he gave her. They unhooked arms and went through the door into the science block. Matt let Chloe step ahead and pulled Jay back into the empty stairwell. 'It'll be OK – whatever it is,' he whispered.

Jay pulled away from him. She wasn't sure she needed any more complications in her life right now.

CHAPTER 3

'Spill,' Matt said, throwing himself on to a kitchen chair and crossing his long legs.

'We're moving to my aunt's,' Jay said flatly. For the second time that day, she attempted to explain what that meant.

Like Chloe, Matt knew a lot about Indian food from raiding her fridge after school, but very little else about Indian traditions and culture. Why would they, when even Jay didn't think of herself as a 'proper' Indian girl?

'Divya – she's in my physics class – she's Indian and she's allowed to do tons of stuff. She's going out with Fred and I've seen them all over each other on the high street,' Matt said.

'Yeah, well Divya's Divya. But Sonia's never been to a single sleepover or even to the cinema with friends. Aunty Vimala's like Sonia's mum; she thinks it's the 1800s,' Jay explained patiently. 'And if we get seen together by one of Aunty Vimala's posse, I'll be in deep trouble – she'll pack me off to India for an arranged marriage.'

Matt's mouth dropped open. 'No way! That doesn't happen any more. Anyway, your mum would never let her do that!'

'Trust me, it happens.'

Jay was worried. Her mum had a way of slipping into being traditional when she was with other Indians. Her dad had always done the opposite.

'And you know we won't be able to hang out in Aunty Vimala's house either – not unless you have a sex change!'

Matt grabbed a scarf and threw it over his shoulders, tossed his head back, and paraded round the flat on his toes, wobbling on imaginary stiletto heels, his narrow hips swinging exaggeratedly from side to side. 'Darling,' he said, in a voice several notches higher than his normal baritone, 'have I ever shown you how good I look in drag?'

She burst out laughing. 'You're gonna have to do a whole lot better than that to fool her!'

The funny thing was that Matt *would* look good

in drag – he looked good in anything. He pulled Jay up from the sofa and wrapped his arms around her. 'Although people may start talking about you and that gorgeous girl you've started hanging out with, and this time they won't be talking about Chloe.'

'Hmm, I wonder what would be worse: Aunty Vimala catching me in the arms of a boy or in the arms of a girl? I think both would be as shocking in her book!'

'Then we'll find a way to hang out,' he said.

The flat door opened and they scrambled to get some school books out before Jay's mum entered the living room.

'Oh hello, Matt. How are you?' her mum asked, before kissing the top of Jay's head.

'I'm fine, thanks, Mrs Sharma. How are you?'

'Very well, thank you. Carry on with your homework,' she said. 'Don't let me disturb you.'

Once her mum had gone through to the kitchen, Jay glanced at her book. 'Oh no!' she whispered.

'What?' asked Matt.

'I was holding my book upside down!'

Her mum hadn't said a word, but Jay knew she never missed the smallest detail.

Jay wasn't keen on Chloe's idea. A double date implied something more than friendship, and as far as Jay was concerned it was better all round if Matt remained her best friend and nothing more.

This was the first Saturday in two years that she hadn't worked in the grocer's. It was strange seeing the shutters down, the sign on the shop door saying *Closed*, the *TO LET* board plastered over *Hope Grocer's*. Instead, Jay spent the day packing boxes while her mum was at work. Matt was calling round for her at four, but he was late, as usual, and they ended up running all the way to the bus stop.

'I bet you did that on purpose,' she said as they ran. 'So we don't have to sit with them in the cinema!' She'd noticed that Matt and Alex didn't get on that well. Matt seemed to put up with him for Chloe's sake.

He grinned wolfishly at her. 'You know what Alex is like! He'll be giving us a running commentary all the way through the film. Just hope they haven't already got us tickets.'

But they had, and the four of them ended up sitting together for the film, with Matt and Jay trying to block out Alex's inane stream of comments.

Afterwards, Matt linked arms with Jay as they walked up to Nando's. The queue was only four deep, but it was still early, and they were lucky to get a table quickly.

'So, you two an item then?' Alex asked, after

they'd ordered their chicken wings. He had his arm round Chloe.

Not exactly the most tactful guy in the world, Jay thought, wondering if Chloe had put him up to it. She laughed it off, taking a sip of her Coke to hide her embarrassment. But Chloe winked at her and Jay felt her cheeks burning.

It got more complicated when Matt gave her hand a squeeze under the table – then he kept hold of it, and Jay's heart did a funny skip. He turned to her and smiled, and she wondered whether this was what she had wanted all along but had been too afraid to admit it.

She prised her hand out of his, but from the way he was looking at her, she knew he'd felt it too. That tingle. Despite her head telling her she'd done the right thing, Jay wished she'd left her hand where it was.

They parted ways with Chloe and Alex after the meal, and Matt walked her home, just as he always did.

'Matt . . .' she began.

'Jay,' he answered. 'I know what you're going to say.'

'You do?' Jay didn't even have the words yet.

'Yes, I do. You're going to say something like: we're best mates and this "us" thing that's happening isn't a good idea. Plus you're moving into Fort Knox, so it's doubly not a good idea. Am I right?'

Jay shrugged. 'Yes, it was going to go something like that.'

'Well, you're wrong.'

'Matt, just listen for a minute.'

He waited for her to continue, his expression suddenly more serious than Jay had ever seen before. 'You know it's more complicated than that,' she said quietly. 'We'll always be best mates, but it would be easier for you to hang out with someone else, someone without all this baggage . . . all these problems and complications.' She felt a tear prick the corner of her eye.

'Remember the first day of school?'

'What?' she asked, surprised. 'Yes.'

'The teacher kept mispronouncing your name, until you told her to just call you Jay?'

Jay smiled. 'The two Ms never let me forget! And they never forgave the teacher for sitting me next to you either.'

'And you refused to speak to me for ages.'

'I didn't speak to anyone for ages, remember?' Her dad had died. She'd just started at a new school. She'd gone from a life of luxury to something entirely different. But Matt knew all that – he'd played the biggest part in coaxing her out of the box she'd locked herself in. 'Anyway, all the girls in the class fancied you, and I had enough problems without having to deal with them hassling me about hogging all your attention.'

'But that's what you're like.'

'I hog all your attention?'

'No, silly. You're always not doing stuff because you don't like upsetting other people. And maybe you're a bit too honest and straightforward, but that's a good thing.'

He took her hand and they started walking again.

'You're not like the others. You're real.'

Jay couldn't resist slapping his arm before she burst out laughing.

'Ouch!' he said, rubbing his arm in mock pain. 'Remind me never to give you compliments!'

When they reached her front door, she quickly stepped back from him and fumbled with the key in the lock. She had to keep some kind of distance between them now that she was moving to Primrose Avenue. Besides, she wasn't ready to venture into unknown territory with him. Not yet.

'See you tomorrow, Matt.'

'Yeah. We said ten, didn't we?'

'That'll mean half past for you then!'

'I'm not always that late,' he objected. 'OK, maybe I am. But I won't be tomorrow,' he promised. 'See ya.'

She watched him walk away, imagining how it would feel to have his lips pressed against hers.

She'd never kissed a boy. She ran up the stairs with an unfamiliar warmth inside her, marvelling at how wonderful it felt just thinking about it.

On Sunday night, Jay tried to change her mum's mind again. 'Can we really not move somewhere else?'

Jay watched her mother take off her glasses and rub her eyes. Her mum looked tired, which made Jay feel guilty – but wouldn't she be more tired when she had to take over all the cleaning and cooking at Aunty V's house?

'No, Jaya. We will move next weekend.'

'Chloe's invited me for a sleepover.'

'Then you will have to say sorry that you cannot go.'

'But why? We can move in during the day, and I can still go over to Chloe's in the evening.'

'No,' her mum said firmly. 'Your Aunty Vimala will be very unhappy if you disappear on your first night there.'

'Why would she care? She's got nothing to do with it,' Jay objected. 'I just need your permission, Mum.'

'Things will be different when we are living there. Remember you are a well-brought-up Indian girl, Jaya,' her mum said. 'Do not shame me in their house. They are proper Indians.'

'Yeah, right, Mum,' Jay said. 'They've lived in

London for years and years and they've got two teenage boys. They're not proper Indians any more. You have to go to India to find proper Indians. Aunty and Uncle are just stuck in a village mentality. Bet the boys are allowed out, and I bet you they eat beef, too,' she added with a smirk.

'Jaya!' cried her mum, scandalized. 'They are strict vegetarians and yes, they are traditional, more so than I have been with you. Do not be so disrespectful. Your Aunty Vimala and Uncle Balji have been kind to help us in this way.'

'"Traditional"? Backward, you mean. Aunty Vimala still thinks that Indian girls shouldn't be allowed to have friends who aren't Indian, Mum! God knows what she's going to think of Matt.'

Jay could almost see her mum biting her tongue. It wasn't exactly the first time they'd rowed about this.

'Do you think it will be acceptable for a boy to visit you in your aunty's house?'

Jay was seething. 'Me and Matt are just friends! He's my best friend.' Her mum gave her a look. 'Anyway, didn't you and Dad rebel against your parents?'

'It was not a rebellion, Jaya. We met in college and fell in love. He was from a good family.'

'But your parents didn't approve. Dad told me. That's partly why we never went back to visit them.'

'Jaya, life was very different in India then.'

'So why are you trying to make it difficult for me here in London? Are you saying living with Aunty V is going to be like living in India then?'

'No, but –'

'Well, I'm not going to be a prisoner in their house, Mum!'

Jay stormed out of the room and slammed the door.

'Um, this door wasn't here the last time I came, Auntyji,' Jay ventured.

They'd bid farewell to the flat, and as they walked through the pillared entrance of 42 Primrose Avenue, Jay had bid farewell to freedom too. Her aunt led her straight towards what had been a coat cupboard and down the stairs to what Jay knew was a dark, creepy cellar.

There had been nothing down there before apart from empty boxes and two large chest freezers full of ready meals from the company that Uncle Bal used to own.

Aunty Vimala turned to Jay with a beaming smile, the heavy gold necklace at her neck straining under her extra chins. She pinched Jay's cheek hard, the way aunties do. 'You will be so surprised with what we have done!'

She led Jay to the bottom of the steps, past the utility room and through the narrow corridor. 'See, you have your own bathroom here.' She pointed to the door on the left. 'And here is the new gym room,' she said, her voice choking up with pride.

It took Jay a few moments to take in the unexpected sight of the shiny wooden floors, the glinting chrome, the treadmill, bike, rowing machine and the racks of dumb-bells along a row of mirrors. There was even some natural light from a bank of windows set at the top of the far wall. Surely Aunty Vimala wasn't proposing she sleep in here?

Her aunt was waiting for her to say something. 'Wow! It's – it's amazing,' she managed.

'All Deven's idea. He is such a good boy, studying hard at university, but he insisted on designing this room himself.' Her aunt gave her a stern look before adding, 'You may use the equipment if you take care of it, Jaya, but I am sure you will be too busy with your studies.'

'It's OK. I do enough sports at school.' Jay was surprised her aunt hadn't left all the plastic coverings on the shiny chrome machines to keep them safe.

'But this is for you, Jaya.' Aunty Vimala pulled her across the gym to a door at the far end. 'Neela has a room in the attic, and this,' she said, opening the door with a flourish, '. . . will be your room.'

Jay had assumed she would be sharing a room with her mum, and the thought of being stuck down here on her own – in the furthest reaches of the house, with her mum two floors away – was disturbing.

The room had obviously served as a store room, there was still a stack of boxes in one corner. It was furnished with a collection of shabby second-hand furniture. There was a single bed in one corner, a bedside table, a desk, a wardrobe and a chest of drawers. The sludgy-brown carpet tiles covering the floor and the grubby coat of grey paint on the walls did little to disguise the room's bleakness.

It wasn't exactly a dark, dank dungeon with iron bars across the windows, but it did feel like a prison – especially with Aunty Vimala's hand clamped, vice-like, on her arm. She was waiting for Jay to be utterly grateful, and Jay, bearing her mum's admonition to 'be nice' in mind, smiled at her aunt and whispered an overawed: 'Thank you so much, Auntyji. You're so kind to do this for us.'

Satisfied, her aunt said, 'It is the least we can do, Jaya. I know it has been a difficult few years for you and your mother.'

And where were you all that time? Jay wanted to ask. Where were any of you?

In a sudden show of affection that took her by surprise, Aunty Vimala threw her arms round Jay and hugged her. 'Everything will be good now, Jaya. Do not worry. We will look after you. I will leave you to unpack. Come upstairs when you finish, and I will show you where everything is,' she added as she left.

Jay sat down on the bed. Had she been unfair to her aunt? Maybe it wouldn't be too bad here after all. Perhaps Aunty Vimala wouldn't mind Chloe coming over now and then. But of course Matt would still be a no-no.

Jay glanced up at the narrow windows that looked out towards the gardens. There was a side gate just round the corner, where the bins were kept. It was a damn shame the windows weren't just a little bit wider – wide enough for her or Matt to squeeze through.

Ash staggered in, under the weight of a box of books. 'Where do you want it?' he asked, trying to balance the box with one hand while hitching up his jeans with the other. Beads of sweat lined his upper lip, which wasn't surprising as this was his fourth trip down to the cellar, laden with heavy boxes. She'd offered to help, but he had insisted.

'Just dump it over there, please.' She had almost finished arranging the bricks and planks of wood she had salvaged from a skip into a bookcase. 'What do you think?' she asked, wiping the dust on her jeans.

'We've got some bricks at the bottom of the garden if you want a bit more space between the shelves. I'll smuggle 'em in if you like.'

'Thanks, Ash. That would be great. If you put them outside that window, I can reach them if I climb on the desk. That way your mum won't know a thing.'

Ash grinned at her. 'You're a fast learner. Oh, I meant to tell you – we've got wireless, so I'll give you the key code for it.'

'Don't worry about it. I haven't got a laptop.'

His eyebrows shot up, disappearing under his mop of dark hair. Ash's passion was computer games, so it must have been shocking beyond belief for him to encounter someone who didn't even own a computer.

'No worries. I've got an old laptop. You're welcome to use it. There's nothing wrong with it,' he added quickly. 'I mean, it's fine for school stuff, just no good for gaming. I'll set it up for you and bring it down.'

'Cheers, Ash.' Jay's mobile bleeped at her twice in quick succession. It was Chloe asking if she could come over for the sleepover and Matt asking if she wanted to come over to his.

'You're popular,' Ash remarked.

Jay looked up at him, thinking he wasn't half as shy as he used to be. 'Just friends wanting me to meet up with them tonight. Do you think your mum would be OK with that?'

'What she doesn't know won't hurt her,' Ash replied. He glanced over his shoulder as though he expected his mum to walk in at any minute. 'As long as she doesn't catch you coming in late,' he said, his voice lowered.

'I haven't got a key.'

'Take mine. Give it back to me tomorrow and I'll get one cut for you.'

'Thanks, Ash. You're a star!'

'I'll bring the laptop down in a bit,' he said, before leaving.

Then Uncle Bal came padding down in his slippers. He gave her a sideways hug, the way Indian men do, before sliding a fifty-pound note into her hand, with the whispered words, 'If you need anything for your room.' He put a finger to his lips. It looked as though everyone kept secrets from Aunty Vimala – even her husband, the great Indian food tycoon.

Jay opened her mouth to refuse, but he gave her a mock-stern look over his glasses. 'Consider it a very late birthday present for last year,' he said, which made Jay smile because in a couple of months it would be her next birthday – her fifteenth.

'Thank you so much, Uncleji, that's so generous.'

He patted her on the shoulder. 'It is nothing, Jaya. If I had known earlier,' he began, but then stopped with a small shake of his head. He smiled and said, 'No matter. There will be plenty of time to talk. I will leave you to finish your unpacking. I hope you will be happy here, Jaya.'

Jay unpacked her boxes of books before making up her new bed and hanging her clothes. When it was all done, she stood back and surveyed her new room. She felt a bit more positive. It still looked desperately sad, but it definitely had potential. It needed brightening up with some posters, some cushions and a very large rug to cover the awful brown carpet tiles. She'd keep a lookout in the charity shops.

This was her new home. She had to make a go of it – for her mum, and for herself. There were tons of downsides – like losing her freedom and not being able to hang out with her friends as much. And Matt. But maybe that was just as well.

She would miss him – his company, his smile and the way he made her laugh. She would try out the windows later, and see if she couldn't just about squeeze through them.

Living here might not turn out to be so bad after all, she thought. As long as she stayed out Aunty V's way.

CHAPTER 4

That first day passed quickly. Life in Primrose Avenue revolved around mealtimes, and Aunty V made it pretty clear from the outset that Jay and her mum were expected to cook, serve, wash up and tidy up. That was the price of her magnanimity in letting them stay there rent-free. Her mum was right – they would save a fortune living here for a while.

But, to Jay, losing her freedom would always feel like a heavy price to pay.

On the first night, after the kitchen had been tidied up and Aunty Vimala and Uncle Balji were ensconced in the living room and her mum was upstairs in her attic room doing coursework, Ash came down to the cellar, bearing gifts.

'OK, here's the laptop.' He placed it on the desk and booted it up. 'It's pretty straightforward to use, but give me a shout if you've got any probs.' He dug into his pocket and pulled out his front door key. 'That's for you too.' He pushed his glasses up his nose. 'Um, the old dears usually go up to bed by ten thirty, but their bedroom's at the front of the house, so just be careful when you're coming back.'

Jay took the key from his outstretched hand. Freedom, she thought, smiling. Matt's house was a mere ten-minute walk away.

Ash hesitated in her doorway. 'Is your mum OK about you going out?'

'Usually, yeah. Why?'

'Think mine might be a bit more strict about it. I mean, with you, you know,' he mumbled, embarrassed.

Jay knew exactly why he was embarrassed. There were rules for him and very different ones for her. It was an Indian thing. 'Cos I'm a girl, you mean.'

Ash shrugged. 'I guess so.'

'Looks like I'll have to do a lot of sneaking around then.' It wasn't something she was used to. She had always been pretty upfront with her mum.

After Ash left, Jay tapped out a quick text to Matt, grabbed her bag, shut her bedroom door and snuck up the stairs. She could hear the TV in the living room from the far side of the hallway, and what sounded like her uncle snoring. She crept up to the door and opened it slowly, wincing at the loud creak, stepped through and pulled it shut carefully. Then she wrote her mum a text, saying she had gone bowling with Chloe and that she would be back by eleven.

As she pressed send, she realized that this was the first time she had told her mum a real lie about where she was going. Jay had a horrible feeling it was going to be the first of many lies.

Her phone beeped almost immediately. Her mum was livid, but she had expected that. She sent her back lots of kisses and promises that she would be careful. Then she sent a text to Chloe saying that if her mum were to ask then to say they were out bowling. Chloe wouldn't mind covering for her. She turned her phone off, slung it in her bag and jogged all the way to Matt's.

'That was easy,' he said, when he opened the front door.

'You think?' She knew that if she switched her phone back on there would be several angry texts from her mum, and probably a few voice messages too.

But it was worth it for a couple of hours away from the grimness of her cellar room. Matt's older sister, Susie, had her boyfriend John over and they hung out with them in the kitchen, playing music and watching videos on YouTube.

'Sorry about this afternoon, Matt, but there was no way I could get out. Did I miss anything?' They had been meant to go to the cinema again with Chloe and Alex, but Jay knew she wouldn't be allowed out.

'Not much,' Matt replied, tossing teabags into four mugs and pouring boiling water over them. 'We were too late to get tickets for the new Marvel film, so we ended up watching some lame romcom that Chloe wanted to see.'

'And you actually managed to sit through it?'

'It was a real struggle.'

'I'm surprised you didn't just leave them to it.'

'Well, I couldn't really. Alex didn't show up, so . . .'

'Oh.' Jay's heart dropped like a stone. She grabbed two of the mugs of tea, almost spilling them in her haste to turn away from Matt. 'There you go,' she said, handing them to Susie and John. She didn't like the way she felt about Matt and Chloe going to the cinema together. Alone. And Chloe had known she wasn't going to be there. It was almost as though . . . But Jay couldn't bear to finish the thought.

Matt placed her mug of tea in front of her and sat down, reaching for her hand across the table. 'I won't be doing that again. I didn't know Alex had bailed on her before I got there.'

She gave him a half-smile and shrugged as though she had no feelings about it one way or the other. But she did have feelings, and they were churning away inside her. She'd been in No.42 for one day and look what had happened!

But what actually had happened? Nothing much, was the answer. Besides, Chloe was her friend.

'It felt weird without you there,' he said.

She knew it was silly, but she was glad he said that. That little spark of jealousy she felt for Chloe was probably more to do with the freedom Chloe took for granted, Jay realized.

'You know, I think Chloe and Alex are having problems. Has she said anything to you?'

Jay thought about it for a moment. Chloe hadn't said a word, but recently all she ever did was complain about Alex. Jay had been too wrapped up in her own problems to notice. On Monday, she would ask her what was going on.

At eleven, Matt walked Jay back to Primrose Avenue. 'There's no one around,' he said, throwing his arm around her shoulders. 'Unless your aunt has got spies with night vision.'

'Knowing her, she probably has. I don't know how, but she seems to be plugged in to all the local gossip.'

'Would you rather I walked ten paces behind you then?'

'No,' she said, laughing. 'That'll look even more suspicious!'

They parted ways before they reached No.42. 'See you tomorrow, Jay?'

Jay shook her head. 'Not tomorrow. I have to go to the temple with my mum, remember?'

'God, yes. Sorry. I'd completely forgotten. Hope it goes OK. I mean . . .'

'It's OK. Dad's been gone a long time.'

'See you on Monday. Call for me – I'm on the way to school now.'

'Yeah, I will.' She watched him walk away, and then turned and headed up the drive.

The lights were off in the front bedrooms. Jay hoped that meant everyone had gone to bed. She put Ash's key in the lock and opened the front door slowly. A small light was on in the hallway, but otherwise the house was in darkness. She shut the front door and tiptoed across the hall to the stairs down to the cellar. Once she was back in her room, she switched on her phone. Just as she thought, there were loads of texts from her mum.

There was also a text from Matt. All he had written was *xxx*.

A little glow spread through her as she padded across the gym to the bathroom, to get washed and brushed. Back in her room, she picked up a book and read until, eventually, she drifted off to sleep with the bedside light on and the book open in her hands.

'But nothing fits!' Jay threw her Indian suits down in despair. She hadn't worn any of them for years.

'Then borrow something from me,' her mum snapped.

'No, thanks. I'll wear trousers and a top.' She pulled out a pair of leggings and an embroidered floaty Indian-style top she'd got from Monsoon.

'Don't forget a *chunni* to cover your head. I'll wait upstairs.' Her mum shut the door behind her as she left.

A row with her mum hadn't exactly been the best way to start the day – especially today of all days. Plus, Jay had been grounded for a month for going out last night. God, a whole month stuck in the dungeons of Primrose Avenue. The thought was unbearable; the reality would be far worse.

Their visit to the temple passed in a blur of tears and anger that Jay fought to keep under control. She hadn't realized it, but her dad's death still felt raw.

She'd spotted her old matron from St Monty's – Mrs Anandhati – at the temple, sitting on the other side, a few rows down. Jay rewrapped her *chunni*, trying to hide her face from her. As Mrs Anandhati got up to leave, Jay turned her face away. Luckily the temple was full, and her old matron didn't notice Jay hiding. But seeing a face from her past was a painful reminder of a time when

Jay's life had been perfect. She'd taken it all for granted then, and she vowed she would never take anything for granted again.

As for her mum – what did she think Jay had been doing the past few years, while she was out working her two jobs? Jay had been forced to grow up fast, and being independent and free to make choices was an intrinsic part of it.

But her mum had already taken a bit of that freedom away from her this morning.

And then Aunty V went a step further in the evening, as she cooked dinner with her mum.

They were presented with a long and detailed list of chores and rules by a very sheepish Aunty V.

'I have not mentioned it before because I do not like to complain, but my back is becoming more painful, and sometimes the arthritis is so crippling I can barely even lift a cup of tea to my mouth,' Aunty Vimala explained with much sighing. 'Yes, it is a lot to ask of both of you, but the housework and cooking has become such a struggle for me. And God in his wisdom,' she raised her palms upwards to the skies, 'did not see fit to bless me with daughters.'

'I am so sorry, Auntyji. I had no idea you were in such agony,' Jay said, with feeling. Her mum shot her a look, but Jay chose to ignore it. 'You cover it up so well.'

Aunty V's beautifully shaped eyebrows puckered into a frown. Jay could tell she wasn't sure how to take her comment, but before either of them could say anything, Jay added, 'Don't worry. Mum and I have everything under control. Why don't you go and put your feet up?'

Aunty Vimala smiled, assured that Jay's words were meant sincerely. 'Thank you, *beti*. You are a very good girl. And did I tell you how nice your hair looks when you plait it like that? When I was a young girl, my plait was as thick as yours.' Aunty V sighed heavily. 'Now, there is very little left.'

Jay had only plaited it because she'd had no time to straighten it with her tongs that morning. Plaiting it was the only way to keep her long, thick, curly hair under control. Jay beamed insincerely at her aunt. 'Thanks, Auntyji. Now off you go and rest those weary feet.' Her mum was still giving her a look, and Jay knew she'd get it from her soon.

'Please do not make fun of her, Jaya. I do not want any problems,' her mum said, right on cue, when the door had clicked shut behind Vimala.

But staying out of Aunty V's way wasn't going to be easy, unless Jay zipped her mouth shut and restricted herself to her cellar room.

'Don't panic, Mum. I won't make problems. But some rules are meant to be broken – and some just shouldn't be made in the first place.'

'This is your aunty's house, so it is natural that she would have ground rules for her house guests.'

'I know, Mum. But there's sorting out ground rules and there is plain taking the piss. I know which –'

'Jaya!' her mother hissed.

So much for zipping my mouth shut, thought Jay. 'Lighten up, Mum. She didn't hear me.'

But her mum didn't lighten up. She did quite the opposite. Everything became deadly serious.

After two weeks of being grounded, Jay pleaded with her to reconsider the ban and let her go out. Everyone was going bowling and Jay really wanted to join them.

'You should have thought of that when you went sneaking out at night.'

'But, Mum, please.'

'No,' her mum said, flatly refusing. 'Actually, the ban is not just for one month, but two months, and then I may think about relaxing it a little.'

Jay resisted the impulse to object and clamped her mouth shut. It was better not to say anything when her mum was in such a foul mood. Her mum would relax the ban within a week or two. Jay was sure of it. But when the month had ended, the ban still stood. Jay's evenings dragged on in what felt like solitary confinement in the cellar, and the weekends were worse, with no school to fill the bulk of the day. There were no distractions in the house other than chores, and her mum rarely ventured down to spend time with her.

Jay spent her evenings alone, her only companions her homework, books from the library, and her phone – until her prepaid credit ran out. The Wi-Fi signal was terrible in the cellar, so Snapchat and WhatsApp, and all the things that would have given her a lifeline, were out of reach. She could download stuff on to the laptop to watch, but that meant spending time in the kitchen with the threat of Aunty V coming in and asking her to make tea, or put a load of washing on, or iron a sari, or some chore or other. Aunty V always found some little task that needed doing. Reading was always Jay's passion, and now it became her solace and her escape. She'd picked up *Tess of the D'Urbervilles* again, even though Matt kept telling her to stop reading it because it was all doom and gloom.

After another week, Jay knew she had to do something, before she either went mad or sank into depression. She had to find a way to be free of Primrose Avenue for at least one day a week. She wished with all her heart that Mr Hope hadn't sold his shop – working there had been a godsend. He'd loved chatting, and he was full of stories. *He must have been lonely too*, she thought with a pang. Mr Hope wasn't there any more, but she would find something else to do.

So after school one day, she went to the supermarket and got herself a weekend job, stacking shelves. She announced it over dinner.

'And I'll get a discount, too, Auntyji. It's only ten per cent, but it'll help,' she said. Jay noticed her mum's pursed lips and the look in her eye, but Aunty Vimala was over the moon at the prospect of the discount.

'I will send Ashok down in the car to pick up the shopping bags, Jaya,' Aunty Vimala continued, beaming at her. 'She is such a responsible girl, Neela. You should be proud of her.'

'As long as it doesn't interfere with her studies,' Mum said tersely. 'That is the most important thing.'

'If that happens, you must stop immediately,' Uncle Bal said. 'There will be plenty of time to work when you are older, Jaya.'

She knew her uncle meant well but she'd had enough of people giving her lectures.

'She is a clever girl, aren't you, Jaya? I am sure she will manage.' Aunty Vimala smiled benevolently at her and Jay smiled sweetly in return, happy she had got the green light so easily.

It was easy to say she was working until eight when in reality she finished at five. Ash came and picked up the shopping at five, which she told him was her tea-break, but as soon as he had gone, she went over to

Chloe's or Matt's, or met up with them somewhere.

The weeks passed, and as they passed, her mum changed. There was a meekness about her now, which Jay found baffling at first, then annoying, and then sickening. Her mum never said no to anything Aunty Vimala asked, and Aunty Vimala was a very demanding person, and she never came down to the basement, and as Jay rarely spent any time upstairs, they hardly saw each other – except when they were busy cooking dinner for everybody. At least in the flat they had spent most of their evenings together watching TV, eating together, talking, or just being together. But here, the distance between the attic and the basement grew bigger on a daily basis – as did the gulf between her and her mum.

CHAPTER 5

'Be down in a mo,' Matt called from the upstairs window.

Jay groaned. Matt was always running late and today was no exception. She couldn't help feeling dispirited. The day hadn't exactly started off the way she had expected, and it wasn't getting any better. She'd bounced up three flights of stairs to her mum's room, feeling happy and excited, but her mum had already disappeared off to work. It was the first time in Jay's memory that her mum hadn't woken her up with kisses on her birthday. Today, she hadn't even said 'Happy Birthday'.

Jay slumped down on the wall outside Matt's front garden. The spring sun was out and it warmed her skin. She pushed her dull, brown knee-length socks down to her ankles and hiked the regulation knee-length school skirt up a few inches, to make the most of the sunshine. A snazzy black Golf pulled over to the kerb and came to a stop directly in front of her. She recognized it instantly and her heart began to beat a little faster. The car window slid down, and Ash leaned out and waved. Jay glanced back, praying that Matt wouldn't come flying out of his front door right then.

'Hi, Jay. Can I give you a lift? I'm going past your school.'

Jay discreetly pulled the hem of her skirt down, suddenly feeling self-conscious and then hating herself for feeling that way. 'Thanks, Ash, but it's OK. I'm waiting for a friend.'

He glanced behind her towards Matt's house, the engine revving gently.

'See you tonight,' she added, desperately wishing he would leave. But Matt chose that precise moment to come bounding out of the house, singing 'Happy Birthday' at the top of his voice. He grabbed her from behind, spun her round, and, before she could stop him, he kissed her.

Jay struggled out of his arms, panicking. 'What the hell are you doing?' she cried.

'Happy Birthday!' He grinned and leaned in to give her another kiss, but she pushed him away and glanced back anxiously. Ash's car was already moving off down the road. Her heart sank. He'd seen everything.

She turned back to Matt, her eyes flashing with anger. 'You stupid idiot! I'm in deep shit now!' she shouted.

'What are you talking about?'

'That was Ash in the car.'

'So? What's the big deal? He's not going to say anything. Why would he? Christ, Jay, stop being so paranoid all the time, will you?'

'I'm not being paranoid,' she yelled, storming off down the road.

Although she had every right to be paranoid. Why couldn't he just stick to the rules? She brushed a tear away as a disturbing thought struck her: if he wasn't going out with her, if he was going out with someone – someone like Chloe – he wouldn't have to stick to any stupid rules. He was obviously sick of it, but was he sick of her too?

She quickened her pace, tears rolling freely down her face.

'Jay! Jay, stop! Look, I'm really, really sorry. How was I supposed to know that was him? You said he was a bit of a nerd – but that was a cool set of wheels he was driving. Come on, you can't get in a sulk with me on your birthday. Am I forgiven?' he pleaded, running in front of her and going down on his knees, hands clasped in front of him. 'Oh God, I made you cry.'

He reached for her hands, but she stepped back.

'Get up, Matt.'

'Not until you forgive me.' This time when he reached for her hands, she let him. He squeezed them between his. 'I got you a present. Will that help?'

'I suppose it might help a bit,' she replied, mollified. 'Now stand up, will you?'

He stood up and his arm automatically moved to go around her shoulder, but he checked himself and let it drop to his side.

She started walking and he fell into step beside her. 'Look – if you're sick of all this, all these stupid rules, Matt, I'll understand.'

'Well, they are ridiculous, but I don't care. They are what they are and that's OK.'

She turned to look at him. 'Are you being honest, Matt? I mean, if you were with someone else, it wouldn't be like this. You wouldn't have to be so secretive. And she definitely wouldn't yell at you for kissing her on her birthday!'

'Jay, I'm one hundred per cent sure that I don't want to be with anyone else. OK, yeah, there's a major culture clash, but it's not between you and me. It's between us and that daft aunty of yours. We can get around that. In a few years, none of it will matter. You'll be free. We're kind of like Romeo and Juliet –

except without the family feuding stuff.'

'Yeah, I will be free . . . eventually,' Jay sighed. *Just a few more years.* 'Hang on a minute. Romeo and Juliet?'

'You know, Shakespeare's star-crossed lovers? That play we read in English last year?' An ironic smile played on his lips.

'Hilarious, Matt. For a start, you're not seventeen and I'm not thirteen! We're nothing like them.' He was trying to be flippant about it, but she realized that was actually how he saw them, and it shocked her. It also made Jay wonder whether Matt was enjoying the subterfuge and secrecy that shrouded their friendship. She hoped he realized it wasn't just a game – that it was serious, and the repercussions would be horrendous if they were found out.

'Not if you think about it – if you ignore their ages,' he argued animatedly. He brushed away the lock of hair that always fell across his eyes, and fixed those brown eyes on her. 'Romeo was banished, just like me. He couldn't see Juliet and had to do it secretively, and Juliet was being forced into an arranged marriage.'

'Matt, no one's forcing me into an arranged marriage. Not yet anyway.'

'I'm only saying that they had to sneak around, and see each other in secret. We need to find our own secret place too – a quiet, dark corner in a coffee shop or a secluded spot in the park. What do you think?' he asked, his brown eyes twinkling.

Jay's heart skipped a beat. She had been so careful not to let things go beyond holding hands, but today he'd caught her unawares. This was the first time he had kissed her on the lips. She barely remembered how it felt. All she remembered was her fear that Ash had seen them. And she couldn't shake that fear – it stayed with her all day.

At school, the two Ms decided to make her day slide further downhill. They were walking up the corridor towards her, smirking and laughing, but it was too late to turn round and go the other way, so she stuck her chin in the air and carried on walking.

'Your friend's gone and dumped you then?' Marissa asked her. Her lips glistened with so much gloss that they looked radioactive.

'What?' Jay had no idea what they were talking about.

'You mean you don't know?' May said, with undisguised glee. 'Matt and Chloe are going out. Saw them in the cinema a few times.' She winked exaggeratedly. 'A-L-O-N-E,' she spelled out, an inch from Jay's face.

The girl wore so much make up that Jay didn't know how she got away with it.

'Just the two of them!' Marissa added, sticking two

ridiculously long pink-varnished nails up at Jay.

'Get lost,' Jay muttered, stalking off quickly, their laughter ringing in her ears.

She knew it wasn't true. Matt had kissed her that morning. He'd said they were like Romeo and Juliet. He wanted them to find a secret place to hang out.

The two Ms were just jealous. May had known Matt since primary school, where they'd been best friends, and she hated Jay for taking him away from her – even though Jay had done nothing of the sort.

She knew Matt had been to the cinema with Chloe once. Were there other times that she didn't know about? When he wasn't with her, which was most of the time, was he with Chloe?

Matt and Chloe.

It sounded better than Matt and Jay, Jay thought, angry at herself for feeling upset. The two Ms never spoke a word of truth – so why did she believe them today? She threw open the bathroom door and locked herself in a cubicle as the tears began to fall. Her two best friends wouldn't do that to her, would they?

Matt thought Chloe was gorgeous, but then so did everyone else. He'd sat through a romcom – which he hated with a vengeance – for Chloe. Chloe was supposed to be going out with Alex, except Alex never seemed to be around . . . Like Jay. She wasn't around the way she used to be.

Jay dried her tears and headed out to maths. Could her fifteenth birthday get any worse?

'Happy birthday. That's for you,' Ash said, handing her an envelope as she reached the top of the stairs from the basement.

'Thanks, Ash. You didn't have to.' She paused before opening it, glancing around to make sure they were alone. She had to bring it up now or else she would spend the whole evening worrying. 'About this morning . . .' she began.

He held his hand up. 'None of my business,' he said. 'But I would be a bit more careful. If it gets around . . .' He left the rest unsaid, his eyes darting round anxiously.

Jay breathed a sigh of relief, glad she had an ally in the house. She couldn't tell Ash it was the first time she'd been kissed, but she would make sure it didn't happen again. She opened the card, and a gift voucher for thirty pounds fell out. 'Wow. That's really generous, Ash. Thanks! For everything.' On impulse, she gave him a hug.

He was so taken aback he had to take his glasses off to polish them. 'We'd better get in the dining room – your mum's made pizza for your birthday dinner.'

'Bet your mum's not too happy about that!'

Ash grinned. 'No, so we'd better not keep her waiting any longer.'

Jay got pizza and cake on her fifteenth birthday. She also got another fifty-pound note from her uncle and aunt, but most importantly of all she got her mum back for a few hours that evening.

Then Aunty Vimala walked into the kitchen, and everything went pear-shaped.

They had finished tidying away the dinner and were sitting chatting. It felt like old times in the flat, and Jay realized how much she had missed her mum. They used to watch *Strictly* together – her mum loved it. They used to laugh together.

'Neela, did you get the chance to tell Jaya about her uncle's birthday?' Aunty Vimala asked.

'Not yet.'

'Never mind,' Aunty Vimala said, with a wave of her hand. 'I will tell her myself. We have planned a very big function for your uncle's sixtieth birthday next month. It will be here at the house and more than one hundred people will be attending. We will make the food at home – it is so much nicer than getting it from outside, isn't it?' She didn't wait for Jay to respond. 'You must take Saturday off work – maybe even the next two or three Saturdays. There is so much preparation, Jaya, and I know you will want to help repay your uncle's kindness.'

Jay bristled, but before she could reply, her mum interposed. 'Vimala, you did not say the function would be here, in the house. So many people! How will we manage?'

'Of course we are having it here. Where else would we have it? We have plenty of room, and Deven suggested getting one of those marquee tents for the garden. He is organizing that, even though he is so busy with studying. It will be a very fancy event,' Vimala concluded proudly. She smiled so bountifully at them that Jay was sure her aunt thought she'd given them a gift rather than a set of Herculean tasks that would tie them to the kitchen for hours and hours over the next few weeks.

'But, Auntyji, Mum's right. That's a lot of people. Don't you think outside caterers would do a much better job for such an important, fancy occasion?'

'Yes, I did wonder that myself, Jaya, but your mother is such an excellent cook, and we are not made of money,' she added quietly. 'The drinks and some of the starters we will be ordering in, but the snacks and the main course will be homemade.'

'We don't really have time for –' But Jay didn't get to finish her sentence.

'Which is why you must take some time off work to help your mother. You cannot expect her to do this all on her own.' Aunty Vimala smiled bountifully again. 'It would make your uncle very happy.'

It was such an unreasonable request, made in such

a manipulative way, that Jay felt her blood begin to boil as Aunty V continued prattling on about the kind of menu she had in mind. Jay had her words ready – lots of them – but the look her mum shot her was so venomous that she was stunned into silence.

'Of course, Vimala. We will make time for this,' Neela said. 'It will be a pleasure to do this for Balji's birthday.'

But what about your teacher training course? Jay wanted to scream at her. She knew her mum had been skipping days to keep on top of the housework and ironing, and all the other little extras that Aunty V insisted needed doing. If her mum carried on like that, there was no way she would qualify as a teacher this century. And that meant they would be stuck here until Jay left for university.

The door swung shut as Aunty Vimala left the kitchen, and Jay directed her glare from her aunt to her mum. Her mum's hand shot straight up into the air, her palm warding off all objections.

'If that's your way of telling me to speak to the hand, Mum, then forget it. For a start, I can't take Saturdays off to cook for a stupid party. You should have said something. She's so out of order it's untrue!'

'Jaya,' her mother said, interrupting her. 'Please, not now. We will talk about it tomorrow.'

'No! You always say "tomorrow", and then you

never have time. You're always too busy working for *her*. I told you we should have got our own place. How can you stand her? She's so awful to you!'

'Be quiet, Jaya. She will hear you.'

'I don't care! I don't care who hears. Let them all hear – it's about bloody time!'

'Shush, Jaya. I care. We are guests in their house.'

'So let's move out then. This isn't how guests are treated, Mum. We're not her slaves. We have to move.'

'No. We cannot afford it. You know that.'

'Yes we could. We were managing fine before.'

'No, we were struggling, Jaya. We never had any money at the end of the week. I could not save one penny.'

'But I'm earning more now, and I could work Sundays, too. Or maybe do a couple of evenings to help out. I'll do anything. Please, Mum. Let's move. Let's get out of here. I can't stand it here. Please,' Jay implored. She begged and pleaded, did everything she could think of. 'Please, Mum. We –'

'Jaya!' her mum hissed, rage and frustration making her brittle. 'No!'

'But, Mum –'

'Just shut up!' Her mum's hand flew towards her face and Jay flinched instinctively, a small cry escaping her lips. But the slap didn't reach her cheek. It stopped inches away.

Mortified, Neela dropped her hand to her side. They stared at each other from opposite sides of the vast space that had opened up between them.

Jay's face crumpled, and tears sprang to her eyes. Her mum had never, ever raised her hand before.

'Jaya,' her mum whispered. Her face was sad as she reached a trembling, tentative hand across the space, but Jay turned and fled down to the cellar.

Her mum didn't come down that night to apologize, nor the next, or the next. Jay cried herself to sleep every night; nothing could take away the loneliness she felt.

CHAPTER 6

Two weeks later, with just two weeks to go before the party, Jay left her Spanish lesson when the end of school bell sounded, and went to look for Matt. He'd asked her over after school, but she'd been given a shopping list by Aunty V, which meant no free time to sneak off.

She was headed down the corridor to the exit when, through the fire door at the end, she caught sight of Matt and Chloe standing together. She stopped and watched them. Her two best friends were smiling and laughing. Chloe had her head tilted to one side, her wide, blue eyes shining up into Matt's brown eyes. There was no sign of Alex anywhere.

It was strange, like a door opening a crack and allowing her a brief glimpse of another reality. She hadn't seen them like that before. Was it only in her imagination, or did other people see them like that, like a couple? Is that why the two Ms were always smirking at her?

Her heart dipped and Jay turned around to find another exit. She didn't want them to see her, not with tears in her eyes.

An hour later, Jay walked into the kitchen. Her mum was cooking the dinner already. Jay set the bags down and started unpacking them, after muttering hello.

'Jaya, we are going to see *Shanti* at the cinema tonight. Why don't you come with us?' her mum asked.

She was trying to be nice, but Jay found it hard to be nice back.

'It is supposed to be a very good film – not just silly fighting, you know. I heard the songs on the radio and they are so good. I think you might like it.'

Her mum was trying to make amends, in her roundabout way, but neither wild horses nor her mum's guilt were going to drag Jay down to the cinema in the company of her uncle and aunt. 'No thanks. Think I'll pass. The excitement will be too much for me.'

Her mum set the rolling pin down, and took the milk out of Jay's hands so she could hold them. 'Please come with us. I haven't seen you properly and it would be nice to go out together.'

Yes, it would, Jay thought, if it were just the two of them. 'I'd love to, Mum, really I would, but I've got stacks of homework.'

Neela raised her eyebrows in mock shock. 'My goodness, Jaya, is that true?' she said. 'You would *really* love to come with us?'

'OK, that might be putting it too strongly.' Jay found herself smiling. Her mother continued to give her that mock-shocked look. 'All right, all right – are you sure you want the truth? Well, the truth is that I'd much rather stay at home and do *all* the washing and *all* the ironing, and dust every surface in the house and polish all the silver, than have to sit through three hours of tragedy piled upon tragedy. Happy?'

'No, I am not happy. Maybe I will stay at home and keep you company, *beti*.'

That would have been nice, but to deny her mum three hours of her favourite film star, Shah Rukh Khan, would have been tantamount to torture. 'It's OK, Mum. It's nice they asked you. Go and have fun, if you can – they're hardly the life and soul of the party.'

'Jaya! Shush! They might hear you,' her mum hissed at her, but there was a smile on her lips.

As if on cue, the kitchen door swung open and Auntyji came rolling in. The smile vanished from Neela's lips.

'What is all this?' Aunty Vimala blustered angrily.

'What is so funny?'

She sounded exactly like Mrs F, the deputy head, who also had an incongruously big, booming voice, which she used to full effect when she caught any of the kids doing something they shouldn't. Jay couldn't resist turning her back and sticking her tongue out. Her mum pointedly ignored her, and adopted her usual dutifully meek submissiveness.

'Oh, we were just being a little silly. That is all, Vimala.'

'Silly? Silly? You think there is time for silliness, Neela? The film will start at 8pm promptly, whether we are there or not. Where is the food? Is it not ready yet? We will get terrible indigestion if we have to eat it too fast.' She patted her chest as though the mere mention of the word had already given her heartburn.

'Yes, it is ready. I'm just going to serve it,' Jay's mum replied, reaching for the ladle. Dhal was poured swiftly into bowls, dotted with knobs of butter and sprinkled with fresh coriander leaves. Rotis were buttered and wrapped in foil to keep them warm. Her mum scurried around the kitchen under Auntyji's beady eyes, and all Jay wanted to do was to scream at them both. Instead, she decided to slink off inconspicuously. She'd eat later – after they had gone.

'I don't want any of this silliness at the party, Neela. We will have so much to do. And where are you going,

Jaya?' Her aunt caught hold of her arm firmly.

'I'll eat later, Auntyji. And don't worry about the tidying up, I'll do it when I've finished my homework.'

Just when Jay thought she knew her aunt well, Vimala did or said something that surprised her.

'Homework – always homework, Jaya. Leave it for one day and come with us to the film,' her aunt said. 'It will be my treat.'

'Thanks, Auntyji, but maybe another time. I've really got to do work on some assignments I need to finish for school.' Jay prised herself out of her aunt's grip. 'Enjoy the film,' she added as she shot out of the kitchen.

By the time her uncle's car pulled out of the driveway, Jay had finished cleaning the kitchen and was back downstairs in her room, pulling on her trainers and grabbing a jacket, before heading back upstairs. It was only seven thirty and it was still light outside, so she didn't text Matt to come up to the house for her. The film wasn't due to finish before eleven and it would take them another twenty minutes to get back. She was free till then.

'Jay?'

She was startled for a moment. Jay had thought she was completely alone in the house, but Ash was hovering halfway up the stairs. 'Yes?'

'Are you going out?'

Jay groaned. Did Auntyji have Ash watching her now? 'Yeah. What's it to you anyway?' she demanded. Ash looked so surprised by her tone that she felt sorry immediately. 'Look, I'm sorry. I'm just going to see a friend.'

'I thought I should tell you.' He was hesitant now. He dug his hands into his pockets and looked at his feet.

'Tell me what?' she prompted, wondering why he was so nervous.

'It's not me, just so you know.'

'Ash, spit it out, will you?'

He pushed his glasses up and his eyebrows shot up, but she didn't feel like laughing this time. 'Some people have noticed you, um, hanging out with – well, certain friends.'

'So? It's not a crime, you know!' She may have sounded like she didn't care, but inside she was suddenly scared.

'I'm just warning you. That's all.' He turned to go back up to his room.

'Hang on a minute, Ash. What do you mean? What people?'

'Look, it doesn't bother me. But Deven, he's got mates here, and they all went to Kingswell Secondary. They know kids there. I'm just saying that with my dad's party coming up, you should be more careful. I know Suresh and a couple of his mates saw you. They told me when I went to deliver the invitations for the party.'

'And what did you say?' Jay asked, her heart thumping.

'I told them they were wrong, it must have been someone else. They said no, that it was definitely you they saw kissing a – a *gora*.'

It would only take one of Deven's friends to mention it to their parents and the story would be all over Kingsbury in a matter of days. Then it would just be a matter of time before it reached Aunty Vimala's ears. And Jay's mum would be livid.

'Shame!' they would scream in her face. 'Shame, *besti*, how could you dishonour the family? How can we hold our heads up in society?'

She'd never, ever, be allowed to leave the house again, unless it was to be packed off to India to get married. She would run away if they tried anything like that. But they wouldn't, would they? Jay had heard stories of it happening, of girls being locked up and drugged and forced into marriage. Her mum wouldn't let it happen, she was sure of it. But, then again, her mum couldn't say no to Aunty Vimala. Not even Uncle Bal could stand up to her.

Jay felt sick. Her only option, apart from running away, was to deny it all. 'Thanks for letting me know,

Ash. They can say what they like. It's none of their damned business!'

Ash took a step down the stairs towards her. 'Are you all right, Jay?'

'What do you care?' She turned her face away, tears threatening to make a fool of her in front of him. She hated it – hated crying, hated looking so weak.

'If Mum asks me anything, I'll say it's not true. OK?'

Jay steadied herself on the banister, not trusting herself to speak.

'Jay? If I can help...'

She sniffed. 'Thanks, Ash. I have to go now,' she mumbled, and rushed out the front door.

By the time she got to Matt's, reality had sunk in. Jay was in trouble.

'We'll just have to be more careful, like he said,' was Matt's answer to her problems. 'Three more years and then we'll be free to do whatever we want.'

Matt made three years sound like three weeks. He made it sound so simple, so easy, when it was anything but. She could barely make it through a week. And now it was going to be far worse. Every day, when she opened the front door to No.42, she would wonder if they had found out, and what they would do to her if they had.

'You don't understand, Matt.' She got off his bed and paced round the room.

'I'm trying, Jay.'

She turned round. 'That's just it. You wouldn't have to try if you were with someone else.' Her mind flickered to the image of Matt and Chloe after school.

Matt closed the laptop and pushed it away. He beckoned her over. 'Come here.' He patted the bed. Jay perched on the edge of it. 'But there couldn't be anyone else.'

'Why?'

He raised his eyebrows. 'It's a pretty long list of reasons. You sure you want to hear them all? OK then.' He drew her close, so that he was inches away from her face, his eyes gazing directly into her. 'You're so beautiful, Jay.' His voice was husky and low. He caressed her cheek. 'And what's crazy is that you don't know even know it.'

The intensity of his gaze was too much. It made her breathless. She pulled away from him and he must have sensed he'd said too much. 'And you're almost as clever as me,' he added flippantly. Jay punched him playfully, glad that he'd lightened the moment. 'But you have read more books than me, so I'll give you that. What else? Oh yeah, you don't live your life on your phone or on Facebook or Snapchat.'

'Only because I've got a crappy phone.'

'No, because you think it's a waste of time.'

'But you're on Facebook,' Jay said.

'Yeah, and you've seen how many status updates I've ever put up. You can count them on one hand.'

The only time Matt was on social media was with her and it wasn't often. Usually they spent that time laughing at what the other kids in their year were posting, and wondering why on earth they'd want to post embarrassing photos of themselves.

'Right, can we get back to the really important stuff now?' he asked, handing her a record to wipe down before he put it in the vinyl-to-digital conversion deck.

She threw a cushion at him with her free hand. 'Glad you've got your priorities right, Matt.'

'Careful, Jay, these records are worth a fortune!'

Matt had a massive vinyl collection, which he was converting so he could add it to his iTunes library. He was a music geek, Jay thought, watching him fondly. And he thought she was beautiful.

Ten thirty arrived too quickly, and even though Jay knew her mum wouldn't be home until later, she didn't want to risk getting caught. It was dark and Matt insisted on walking her back, so she let him – but only to just out of sight of No.42.

'Jay, you've got to lighten up. Stop taking everything so seriously. Let it all go.'

It was easy for him to say. She hadn't told him about

her mum almost slapping her. It felt too disloyal – she knew how much he liked her mum.

'Come here.' He pulled her behind a hedge and drew her into his arms, and she let him. No one else hugged her any more. She loved the intimacy – the warm feeling that flowed through her when she was in his arms, with her head resting on his chest, listening to the steady thump of his heartbeat.

'Hang in there, Jay. It can't get any worse.' He stroked her hair, and for some reason she started to cry.

'It's OK,' he whispered. He kissed the top of her head. 'Worse comes to the worst, we'll run away. They can't stop us. We'll abscond! Elope. Do people still go to Gretna Green?'

'Don't know, but eloping isn't really going to help,' she said, her voice thick.

'We'll think of something,' he promised.

'I don't know, Matt. I don't know.'

A week later, on the day of the party, she wished she had done just that. Eloped, to live happily ever after in a village near Gretna Green.

CHAPTER 7

It was the eve of the big day and Jay could hear her aunt's shrill screeching as she turned into the drive of No.42. It got louder as she approached the front door. Jay groaned as she put her key in the lock, and hesitated before entering, steeling herself. Her uncle's party didn't start until tomorrow afternoon, but the house was already in mayhem. Clearly her aunt's nerves had reached a frazzled state. Jay waited a couple of moments, hoping her aunt and whoever she was screeching at would move out of the hallway, but no such luck. She cursed her bad timing, and went in.

'No, no, no, I said put them in the storeroom, Ashok! They will get knocked down and broken, with so many children running around the house. And

91

remember what I told you about sending them out into the garden. No children in the house! And I do not want anyone going upstairs. Plenty of bathrooms down here for everyone.'

Poor Ash was on the receiving end. Her aunt was huffing and puffing and red in the face. Jay shrank back as accusing eyes turned on her. Ash gave her a resigned smile of solidarity from behind his mum, before ducking swiftly out of the hallway.

Vimala planted her hands on her hips and Jay braced herself for the tirade. 'So now you come home! Where have you been all this time, Jaya? Come, quickly, put your bag down and help. Did you forget we are having a party tomorrow? No sense in you girls today! Why are you so late?'

'Hi, Auntyji,' Jay said, gritting her teeth while attempting to smile sweetly at her aunt. She toyed with the idea of saying 'Mind your own business, you nosy old battleaxe', but opted for her trusty library excuse. 'Sorry, Auntyji, I had to go to the library as I won't get the chance tomorrow. I'm really sorry. I'm all yours now.'

Her aunt wasn't impressed. 'Help Ashok with these ornaments. Where has he gone? Ashok? Ashok?'

'I'll find him. Why don't you sit down and have a rest?'

'Have a rest? Have a rest?' her aunt boomed. 'Who

will do all the work? There's no time for rest.'

Jay glanced round the hallway – it looked as though they'd only just made a start with clearing the furniture. It was quite a grand hallway, with a huge mirror opposite the door. Beneath it was a long glass-topped marble table covered in family photographs, vases and knick-knacks. A cleaner's nightmare, as Jay knew only too well. She picked up a vase of dried flowers, which looked as if they'd been dead a century or more, and almost dropped it when her aunt shouted, 'Be careful! Don't break anything! Take them to the spare room. And when you have finished, come and arrange the tables. Everyone will be eating outside tomorrow. I want all the plates and cutlery arranged properly. And do not forget the napkins, Jaya, I want them folded in a special way . . .'

After what felt like a lifetime, they took their first break. Jay headed down the hallway with Ash when, through the open front door, they saw a bright red sports convertible swinging into the drive. The driver revved the engine and tooted his horn, just in case anyone had missed his arrival. Next to her, Ash grimaced and mumbled something under his breath.

'Is that Deven?' Jay asked. She hadn't seen him for about three years. He'd changed a lot, although the goatee wasn't doing much for him, she thought.

'Who else?' Ash muttered.

They stepped aside as Aunty Vimala charged past them in her haste to greet her son first. 'My favourite boy!' she called.

Jay noticed Ash's expression had soured. There seemed to be some bad blood between him and his brother, and Aunty V calling Deven her favourite son couldn't have helped.

By now Deven had reached the front door. He stooped down and allowed himself to be enveloped by his mum.

'Deven! My clever, clever boy – finally you are home! We have missed you very much,' Auntyji cried, through sniffs and tears.

Deven replied in the same vein, but without the sniffs and tears. He extricated himself from his mum and promised to meet her in the garden as soon as he brought his bags in. Then he turned to his brother. 'Ash, man, how're you doing, bro?'

'Yeah, it's all good,' Ash replied. 'Still got that car then?'

'It's a beaut! You should trade yours up.' Deven leaned in closer to Ash. 'Girls love it!' He laughed loudly, but Jay saw Ash's mouth tighten, and she wondered whether Ash wasn't more than a little jealous of his older brother.

Then he turned to her.

'Well, well, well,' Deven drawled, 'you've grown, Jay.'

'So have you!' He was much taller than she remembered, almost a foot taller than her, and he'd bulked out considerably.

'Less of the cheek, little cousin.'

'We're not cousins, and I was only being honest.'

He smoothed down his little moustache and goatee. 'Yeah, but you're looking real good, Jay. Bet the boys are falling over themselves to get to you. How old are you now?'

'She was fifteen last month,' Ash said.

'Well, happy birthday, Jay! Sorry I missed it.' Deven kissed her on the cheek.

'Thanks.' The brothers were so different, Jay thought, recalling the first time she'd seen Ash after a few years' break. He'd come to help them move out of the flat and he'd been shy and awkward. Everything about him said 'geek'. Deven was the complete opposite: he was ultra-confident, almost brash, and he had a trendy haircut, designer jeans and a smart shirt. Jay wrinkled her nose – and way too much aftershave. What did he do – wash his clothes in it?

'Look, do you want to get your stuff in? Because Dad's waiting for you in the garden,' Ash said. 'You were supposed to organize the marquee.'

'Yeah, OK, little bro. I'd better not keep the old

man waiting. Here.' He threw the car keys at Ash. 'There's only one bag and it's in the boot.'

He put his arm round Jay's shoulder and led her through the house.

'Hasn't she grown up, Ma?' he said.

'She is a very good girl, Deven,' Aunty Vimala replied, smiling happily through her tears. 'Such a help to me. Jaya, *beti*, go and make some tea for us all.'

Deven eventually sauntered out to the garden to see his dad. After a quick half an hour with his parents, he swanned out to see his friends. Ash was still in a filthy mood, which Jay resolved to ignore. She could kind of see why he was jealous of his older brother – he was better looking, he was his mum's favourite and he had a much flashier car. Jay had been worried about what Ash had said the other night about Deven's friends seeing her with Matt. Petrified, actually. But now she had a feeling Deven would be cool about it.

Ash was just being his usual self – worrying about everything, and making her nervous about nothing.

It was almost eleven when she escaped her aunt's clutches, and even then it was only because of Uncle Balji, otherwise it would have been even later.

'Vimala, that is enough,' he said as he came into the kitchen. He was already in his pyjamas and dressing gown. He placed his hands on Jay's shoulders. 'Look at this girl. She is half asleep on her feet, and Ashok is already sleeping.' He pointed at Ash, who was sat at the kitchen table, rubbing his eyes. 'And how will you host such a big party if you do not have enough sleep too?'

'I want everything to be perfect for your birthday, Balji. So many people coming – the house must be looking its best.'

'It is looking perfectly fine. Let the children go to sleep now. Come.' Aunty Vimala allowed him to lead her upstairs.

Jay headed into the hallway with Ash. He started up the stairs, and then stopped.

'Jay?'

She turned around on the top step of the cellar stairs. 'Yes?'

They could both hear music coming from the cellar.

'Nothing. Good night.' He turned and sped up the stairs.

Jay shrugged. He'd been in a funny mood all night. She was dead tired and ready to crash straight into bed, but someone was in the gym, and that someone could only be Deven. She hesitated, wondering whether to let him finish his workout undisturbed. She could go up and see her mum, only she didn't have much to say to her at the moment – at least, nothing that her mum wanted to hear.

She ducked into the bathroom to get washed first. The music was still playing when she came out, but Jay was too tired to care. She needed her bed.

Deven was sitting on the bench with a dumb-bell in his right hand, his face in a knot of pain and the soundtrack of *Rocky* blaring at full volume around him.

'God help me,' she muttered under her breath – he had dire taste in music.

His eyes lit up when he saw her. 'Jay, my favourite girl! How's it going?'

'Yeah, fine. Knackered!' she shouted over the music, hoping he'd get the message and call it a night.

Deven reached across to the stereo and turned the volume down. 'All done upstairs?' He was breathing heavily. Sweat dripped from his forehead and trickled down his face, making his goatee glisten. He placed the dumb-bell on the floor with a grunt and mopped his face with a damp towel.

'Yeah, for now. So, how did you manage to get out of the work so easily?'

He cocked his head to the side and smiled, ever so sweetly, at her. 'That's how. My mum is a real sucker for a smile and sweet talk.'

'Well, it might work for you, but it's never worked for me – or for Ash.'

'Ash is way too moody – that boy needs to get out

more, have some fun. And you, you're a girl, Jay, and you know the old dear's got strict ideas about girls and their place.'

'Yeah, tell me about it,' Jay groaned.

'I know a good way of getting rid of all that anger. Here, I'll give you a personal training session. This stuff is top of the range gear, you know. Try it – you'll love it. It'll make you hot and sweaty, but it's fun. You like a bit of fun, don't you? What do you say?'

For a second, his tone bothered her. She wasn't sure whether he was referring to what his friends might have told him. Had they told him about her and Matt? She couldn't ask him outright. 'No thanks. We had a good workout upstairs.'

'Yeah, I heard the old dear going on. She can be hard work all right. But her heart's in the right place.' His eyes slid up and down Jay admiringly. 'You've really grown into the cutest looking thing I've seen in a long time.'

'You're all charm, aren't you? Now, hop it, I need my bed.'

'And bossy too! I'm almost done. But the offer's open. Anytime you want. I'll be right here waiting for you.'

Jay was just about to shut her door when he said, 'Oh, one more thing, Jay.'

'Yes?'

'You don't need to worry.'

She frowned. 'Worry about what?'

'I saw my mates tonight. They told me what you've been up to, you know, with that *gora* boyfriend of yours. Who's been a naughty little girl then?'

Jay's heart skipped a beat. He made it sound like she was sleeping around. 'Nothing's been happening.'

'Oh yeah? Not what I heard.' He winked at her. 'But your little secret's safe with me. My friends know to keep their mouths shut. The old dear won't hear about it.'

She breathed a sigh of relief. She'd spent so long worrying, and it had been for nothing. Ash had been completely wrong about his brother and his friends. 'Thanks, Deven, I really appreciate it.'

'No problem.'

At least that was one thing she didn't have to worry about, she thought, as she got ready for bed. Tomorrow was going to be a long day, but, as exhausted as she was, she couldn't sleep straight away.

She reached for her book, and had only read about twenty pages when her mobile beeped twice, so loudly it startled her. The music in the gym had stopped, but she hadn't noticed when.

Jay grabbed her phone, making a mental note to remind Matt never to text anything incriminating – or add any kisses.

Nite, J. Good luck with the party tomorrow xxxxxxxx
She was smiling as she sent her response.

And she was still smiling when she turned out the light.

CHAPTER 8

The promised heatwave had finally arrived. Jay slipped into a pair of shorts and a vest, and stuck her feet into flip-flops. She made some toast and tea and sat in the garden, munching and basking in the sunshine, feeling happy. She had awoken to another text from Matt.

See you at 9 tomorrow morning – less than 26 hours to go! xxxx

She couldn't wait to meet him in the park in the morning. The countdown had begun.

Heat shimmered across the lawn, the morning dew a distant memory, and it was barely half past seven in the morning. This was Jay's favourite time out here, alone and serene in the garden. The bird chatter and the odd pesky squirrel foraging for anything that looked edible were the only interruptions to the quiet. She imagined herself somewhere else – somewhere far, far away, where life was a bottle brimming over with bubbles of laughter and happiness – and, for a while, it worked.

The back door opened and the bubbles popped. She was wrenched back into the real world. But it was only her mum.

'Jaya, you are up already? You should have stayed in bed for longer. It is going to be a very busy day.'

Her mum kissed the top of her head.

'I was hungry, so I got up.'

'Let me make you some more toast,' her mum offered, getting up.

'No thanks, I've had tons. Sit down, Mum. It's going to be a busy day, remember?'

'Yes.' Her mum sighed heavily and sat down. 'It is. In a few hours this garden will be unrecognizable.'

They sat in companionable silence, listening to the bird chorus and the lazy breeze rustling through the leaves in the trees. A few years ago, this was how it had been every summer. Magical.

Jay hadn't thought of it as magical then. Then, it was normal. It was her everyday life and she had never thought it would be any different.

Her mum would be pottering around her vegetable patch, giving a running commentary on what was flourishing and what wasn't doing as well, and Jay would listen with half an ear while she read a book or worked on her tan. Her dad would be clipping the bit of hedge the gardener had missed, or tending the barbecue.

She missed him so desperately. Why did it still hurt this much after three years?

Tears welled in her eyes and a hard lump formed in her throat. Nostalgia was a dangerous thing. If she didn't keep it under lock and key it would consume her.

Jay got her emotions under control before putting her tea down and turning to her mum. There weren't many moments like this, and she couldn't let this one pass without saying something.

'Mum,' she began hesitantly. 'I know you think we need to live here for a while, and I understand why. I know all the arguments . . . I just don't want to do it any more.'

'Jaya –'

'Please, Mum, let me finish.'

The weary slump of her mum's shoulders told her she could continue if she wanted, but that in the end it wouldn't matter. She desperately wanted to take her mum by the shoulders and shake some life back into her – make her realize that what was happening mattered. 'We never see each other any more, haven't you noticed? I – I miss you, Mum. You're acting like you're Aunty Vimala's personal maid! But you're not, and you don't have to be. Can't you see that?'

'I do what I must, Jaya, and I don't mind it, really.'

'But it's not right.'

'It *is* right. Balji and Vimala are helping us, so the least I can do is to show them some respect.'

'Respect? Respect is a two-way thing, Mum,' Jay countered angrily.

'Keep your voice down, Jaya,' her mum whispered, glancing round anxiously. 'I have not asked you to do anything extra, so why are you angry?'

Jay felt like crying. Her mum had been so strong after Dad had died. Where had that woman gone? How could she ever get her back? She knew it wouldn't be by shouting and kicking and screaming, but it was hard maintaining a calm exterior when inside she was boiling over with anger and frustration and – and loneliness.

'Mummy, we had less money when we lived in the flat, but we could be ourselves – and laugh and smile and giggle as much as we wanted. We were together. Don't you remember? We weren't that much more broke than we are now. Can we move, Mum? Please, will you think about it?'

And, as a frown flickered across Neela's face, settling with depressing permanence, Jay knew her mum wouldn't be thinking about their talk. Her mind would already be on what was left to do in the kitchen before the guests began to arrive, and then on to where she would fit in her backlog of coursework, missed due to the weeks of party preparation. Jay's cheapskate aunt had insisted even the Indian sweets be homemade.

'I'm going to leave.' Jay hadn't planned on saying it, but the words slipped out.

'What? And where will you go? Don't be so stupid, Jaya. We cannot leave yet. I know you are finding it hard, but we have saved so little.'

'I don't care about saving! My room is like a morgue. I can't bear it!'

'Then you must try harder.' Her mother's mouth was fixed in a hard line. No matter what Jay said, she wasn't going to waver. 'I do not see the big problem, Jaya. Your room is nice, the garden is lovely. The area is safe and we are fortunate to be living with such a good family. A few more years.'

'What? A few more years? But you said a short while. I can't do it.'

'You have to. You know how expensive renting is.'

'What if we get one of those six-month interest-free credit cards? Then we could switch the balance to another card and carry on doing that until you're assigned your teaching post. That would work. Please.'

Jay's mum shook her head. 'Jaya, after what happened do you think any credit-card company is going to give us a card?'

Jay hadn't considered that. Her dad's business debts had left them bankrupt. No one in their right mind would give them a credit card or a loan.

Her uncle's arrival brought their fruitless conversation to an end. Her mum scurried off to make his breakfast, leaving Jay alone with him. He had the paper in his hands, but didn't seem to be reading it. Her dad used to read the paper aloud at the breakfast table. 'Can you believe some people today, Jaya?' he'd say, with a shake of his head, and then he'd find a funny story to read aloud to her.

Unlike her dad, who was a talker, Uncle Balji was quite reserved. So they sat together in companiable silence until she suddenly remembered the reason for the big party.

'Happy Birthday, Uncle,' she said, getting up and giving him a hug, wincing inwardly as she realized that she'd forgotten to buy him a card or a present.

'Oh, thank you, Jaya. I don't usually celebrate these things. Such a fuss for an old man, but your aunty insisted, and you know your aunty.' He regarded her kindly over his reading glasses, and she gave him a half-smile. 'So how is school?' he asked. 'Ashok and Deven both went to Kingswell too. Deven very much enjoyed it there, but not Ashok. He could not wait to go to college.'

She knew how Ash felt. 'It's OK. I liked my old school better.'

Uncle nodded. 'Yes, but it cost too much money, Jaya. You can get a good enough education here at this school, too. It does not matter where you learn, as long as you have the desire to learn and better yourself. I remember, when I was a very young boy growing up in India, I went to the local village school, and I was lucky – we had the most excellent teachers. We were accepted by good colleges, and fortunately my family could afford to send us to them. After I graduated, I took the opportunity to come here and make a better life. And see,' her uncle raised his hands in the air, 'see what I have managed to achieve? You are a very clever girl, Jaya. I do not have to tell you that there are things in life that you will have to do – whether you like them or not. That is life.'

Jay wondered whether he'd overheard her conversation with her mum. Why hadn't her mum asked him for a loan, instead of rooms in their house? He knew how hard her mum worked, so he'd know he'd get his money back. The arrival of Auntyji put paid to the idea of talking to him about it now. Uncle Balji picked up his newspaper, as Jay's aunt launched into a list of impossibly detailed instructions and ran through the schedule for the day.

'And the cake will be cut at 4 o'clock precisely,' her aunt concluded. 'It is not auspicious to cut it late, so everything must be happening at the proper time.'

'Vimala,' Uncle Bal began, 'do you not think we should be a little more, ah, flexible, with the schedule? It is a party, you know, not a military campaign. I want everyone to relax and enjoy themselves. We want to have fun, don't we, Jaya?'

Auntyji glowered at him until he sighed resignedly and returned to his newspaper. Then she turned her attention back to Jay. 'What will you be wearing today, Jaya? Do you have something nice? You need a proper suit, not a sari because it will just get in the way when you are helping me with the guests.'

'Um, yes, I've got a lovely summer dress I was planning on wearing,' Jay murmured. She picked up her cup and sipped the cold tea to hide her consternation. It hadn't occurred to her that she would have to wear something Indian.

Her aunt didn't notice Jay's silent panic, but, surprisingly, her uncle did. 'Jaya, why did you not tell us earlier? I would have asked your aunty to take you shopping for something new to wear. Is it too late now?' He glanced at his watch. 'No, there is plenty of time. Go to the high street – there are two or three shops there, and you will find something nice in one of them. Here,' he said, reaching into his pocket for his wallet, 'it will be my treat.'

'What are you doing?' Aunty Vimala barked. 'There is no time for clothes shopping now! The guests will be arriving in a few hours.' She tutted at her husband. 'I am sure you can borrow something *appropriate* from your mother.' She stared disapprovingly at Jay's short shorts and vest top.

Jay decided it was time to escape. She headed back to the house, wondering how on earth her uncle could bear to live with such a mean-spirited woman. She snatched the kitchen door open and saw her mum counting off boxes of Indian sweets to give away at the end of the party.

'I've got nothing to wear, Mum.'

'You have plenty of clothes, Jaya.'

'So I'll wear that summer dress I got in the sales.'

'No, no. You must wear Indian today – your aunty will expect it.'

'But the last time I wore Indian clothes was when I was twelve! They'll be tight in all the wrong places and way too short.'

'Suits with a shorter dress and tighter trousers are more fashionable now. There is plenty of length in the trousers – remember how bunched up they are?'

'Mum, I've got boobs now! I'll be busting out of the top of the dresses!'

'I don't have time for alterations, Jaya. When I go up I will find a few suits of mine you can try on. Now let me finish.'

Her mother turned her attention back to the boxes

of *ladoos*, so Jay flounced out of the kitchen, and in her haste crashed straight into Deven. He caught hold of her in his arms before she could backpedal through the swing doors into the kitchen.

'Sorry,' she muttered.

'Don't be. You smell good. Irresistible,' he murmured before releasing her. He looked her up and down, his mouth sliding into a sideways smile, his eyebrow arched suggestively. 'And where have you been hiding those legs, huh? *Sexy!*' he added, leaning in close.

'What?' She was shocked. What had got into him this morning?

'If you want my opinion, tight in the wrong places is a good thing. And as for busting out the top . . .'

It was obvious he'd been standing on the other side of the door, listening to her conversation with Mum. But why? And the way he was looking at her now felt wrong. There was nothing brotherly in the way his eyes slid down her body. Suddenly Jay's shorts felt too short, her vest top too revealing.

She pulled a face at him, and quickly slipped past. Deven went into the kitchen, chuckling to himself. She glared at his back before heading down to the cellar. She gave the treadmill a kick and didn't unclench her fists until she was in her room.

She'd probably been a little naive. He'd been

making comments about how gorgeous she was ever since he'd arrived, but she'd brushed them off. Luckily, she didn't see Deven for the rest of the morning, but she did change into her jeans, despite the heat.

But from that moment on the whole day went spiralling helter-skelter downhill for Jay.

Auntyji put on her sweetest smile to greet her guests, but Jay knew she was in a foul mood because despite all her careful planning, everything was already an hour off-schedule. At least it became easier to avoid her aunt as the house and garden filled up with people. Much to her relief, although the pale-blue silk Indian suit Jay had borrowed from her mum was a few decades out of fashion, she blended in all right.

The heat built up as the day progressed, the sun bringing out the vibrant colours of the women's saris as they sashayed around on spiky sling-backs. To Jay's amazement, they walked, danced, handled their saris, held their glasses of wine and kept their balance, while hordes of screaming children played tag around them. Jay was pretty sure it was wine in their glasses. Her parents had always served wine to the women and 'something stronger' for the men.

Auntyji was still in the Dark Ages, so she had distinctly forbidden alcohol today, but it looked as though the birthday boy had overruled her. Jay caught sight of him on the decked patio, manning a makeshift bar – a cool-box the size of a car boot – and she was oddly proud of him for defying his wife. Uncle Bal was grinning from ear to ear like a big kid, immensely pleased with himself. Her aunt was parked in front of him, arms crossed, glowering thunderously as he attempted to foist a glass of wine upon her.

'Vimala, just take one small glass to celebrate this most special day you organized,' he said coaxingly. She turned her nose up at it and strutted off.

Jay made the rounds of the garden, picking up discarded plastic cups and paper plates, listening to Bollywood music and remembering how her mum used to take her hands and dance round the kitchen, teaching her the steps and the movements, twirling her this way and that. But Jay was younger then. They hadn't danced like that for years.

Jay ran errands to and from the kitchen all afternoon, rearranged the towers of kebabs and tandoori chicken, refilled the plates of samosas and pakoras when they ran low, topped up the pickles and yoghurt and salad and sauces. Dinner was going to be served after the cake had been cut, but she didn't think anyone would have any appetite left for the main course her mum had slaved over all morning.

She felt strangely detached from the whole event, like a ghost gliding unnoticed in the background.

People-watching kept her from dying of boredom. Some of the outfits were stunning: shimmering silks and sequins, beaded and embroidered floaty fabrics in the most fashionable styles. It would have been fun to try some of them on just this once, because when she left No.42, Jay was determined never to wear a sari or an Indian suit again.

There were dancers and a band booked for the afternoon. That was when Deven and his friends showed up, and the volume went up several hundred decibels. She had to be careful now that his friends were here.

The music switched from Bollywood to a more local blend of Punjabi songs. Beer bottles dangling from their upraised hands, Deven and his crew hit the dance floor, shoulders bouncing up and down to the bhangra beat as they swaggered round the women. Deven grabbed his mum and pulled her on to the dance floor and she beamed happily, so proud of her son. The track ended and Deven cast his eye around for another victim. Jay sped off to the kitchen to avoid being dragged on to the dance floor.

Somehow her mum had enlisted the help of several women and, judging by the peals of raucous laughter, they were having their own little party – and it looked much more fun than the one outside. Neela was hot and flushed, but animated and happy too. It lifted Jay's heart. She wanted her mum back – this one in front of her, not the simpering shadow who would return after the party was over. Neela caught sight of Jay standing in the corner and shooed her back outside.

'Go and enjoy the party, Jaya. We can manage.'

Reluctantly, Jay left the kitchen. Her uncle weaved past her, clumsily bumping into people and apologizing with the slightly lopsided smile of a happy, bumbling, tipsy person. It was only mid-afternoon and Jay wondered what kind of state he'd be in when it was time to cut the cake. Aunty Vimala would show him no mercy.

And then Jay's uncle surprised her again. He weaved his way back towards her, bearing a plastic cup, which he thrust into her hand with a slurred, 'Thank you for helping, Jaya. You are a very good girl. A beautiful young lady. Here. We need to get you into the party mood!'

'Thanks, Uncleji.' She took a small sip. It was wine! He was full of surprises today.

Uncle Bal gave her a hug. 'It is nice for us to have a girl in the house. I will come back and make sure you are having a good time,' he said, as he ambled off.

Halfway through the drink, when her head felt like it was about to drift off with the white puffy clouds floating across the sky, Jay topped her glass up with orange juice.

'Hey, Jay.'

It was Ash. He'd dressed up for his dad's party – new shirt and jeans. She hadn't seen much of him so far.

'Come over and join us if you like,' he said.

He must have noticed she was being a wallflower. 'OK. If you're sure.'

She followed him nervously to a group of older teenagers, who she guessed were his friends from college. She felt shy and tongue-tied at first, which wasn't like her, but there were a few girls there, all of them Indian, and they made a big effort to include her. Soon she was smiling and chatting back, and wishing she'd met girls like Radikha, Pinky and Ravvy before. She had been the only Asian girl in her class at St Montague's, and the ones at Kingswell, well, they weren't really her type.

Ash's friends were all planning to go to uni, and, although they got disapproving looks and tongue-clicking from some of the oldies, they just shrugged it off. Their parents weren't strict the way Auntyji was, even if they weren't quite as liberal as her dad used to be. There were thousands of variations and degrees in between the two extremes – it just depended on your luck.

'Bide your time, Jay,' Ravvy advised her. 'Once you're eighteen, don't let anyone stop you doing what makes you happy.'

Jay thought she might ask Ravvy for her number – it was nice knowing someone who understood so completely, but just then the dancers came fluttering on to the dance floor and everyone went quiet.

They were fabulous, all twirling hands, spinning skirts and tinkling bells. At the end of their show, they fanned out into the audience and persuaded people out of their seats to dance. Most of the guests went willingly, even the girls she was sitting with. Ravvy grabbed her hand, but Jay shook her head and pulled away. She watched them for a moment, and then tossed the last of her drink back and slipped down to her room, as the party started up in earnest. She wanted to talk to Matt.

Downstairs, it was cooler but only a little quieter. She kicked off her sandals and lay down on the bed. His mobile must have been switched off, because it went straight to voicemail. She remembered he'd said he might go to the cinema, so she left him a message.

Miss u tons! 15 hrs to go till we meet tomorrow! xxx

She sank back on to her pillow and stared up at the ceiling. Fifteen hours sounded like for ever, but most of the guests would leave by eight or nine o'clock, especially the ones with younger kids. If she got to bed before midnight, that left just five or six hours to get through. She closed her eyes, resting them for a moment. The wine had made her drowsy, but there was surely no danger of her falling asleep – not with that racket going on right outside her bedroom window . . .

Gradually, the loud bass of the music became more distant and the sound of voices and laughter faded into the background, as she drifted off to sleep.

CHAPTER 9

Jay awoke with a start. The music was deafening, loud and fast, with a heavy bass beat. It was so loud it sounded as if it was coming from just outside her door and not from the other end of the garden, where the band and the sound system had been set up. Drunken voices were yelling the lyrics to a Punjabi bhangra song, out of time with the music. She sat up slowly, grimacing at the sudden pounding in her head, and checked the time. It was nine o'clock! She had come down to her room at about six, which meant she'd been asleep for three hours. Three whole hours! Her aunt was going to kill her for doing a disappearing act when there was work to do. But if they had missed her, they would have come down and woken her up.

Her head was splitting. There were painkillers in the drawer of the bedside table. She rummaged around blindly, but night was falling and she couldn't see a thing. She groaned as she swung her legs over the side of the bed. She needed to switch the lamp on, even though the glare would blind her. But as she reached for the switch, she paused.

A sliver of light outlined her bedroom door. She listened, hand poised on the switch, suddenly very wide awake and alert. The music and the loud drunken voices weren't coming from the garden. They were coming from somewhere much closer. The gym.

Deven. But this time he wasn't alone – he'd brought his crew down with him. They were trashed when she'd last seen them in the garden. They'd had a drink on the go even when they were dancing, sloshing it back like water, and spilling it all over the place. God only knew what kind of state they were in now.

She was trapped – only an idiot would venture out there without heavy protection. Not for the first time did she wish her door had a lock and a bolt, and maybe a hefty iron bar she could use to barricade herself in. She might have felt a lot less vulnerable then.

Jay glanced round. Her room was in semi-darkness, but she didn't need to see clearly to know there was nothing that would serve as an effective barrier if they decided to hassle her. There was a flimsy chest of drawers – two of the drawers kept coming apart. The table that served as her desk was only still standing because it was propped up on one side with books, the broken leg leaning against the wall beside it. The chair was a standard lightweight plastic garden chair, which if you leaned back in it a couple of degrees, put you in danger of tipping and splitting your skull open. And that was it.

There were cheap bedsits that came better furnished.

They couldn't know she was in her room, which was good but not much help when she needed to get out. She needed the loo and she wanted to see her mum – maybe even sleep in her room tonight, because the party in the gym was bound to go on till late.

During a lull in the music, Jay heard voices arguing over which track to play next. She tiptoed to the door, and without having to press her ear to it, she heard Deven's voice. She had harboured the flimsy hope that maybe it was Ash and his friends. But, no. The choice of music alone should have told her it wasn't. They wouldn't have been listening to this kind of bhangra music at top volume.

Deven's voice was the loudest by far, but there were others. She couldn't work out how many. She shuddered. After bumping into him that morning, the last person she wanted to see was Deven. Or any of them. Ash would be sober, but there was no way he would be hanging round with his older brother and his Neanderthal friends.

It was better to stay put for now.

The music started up again, and Jay sank, dejectedly, to the ground. She pressed her back against the door, and drew up her knees. It was sheer madness to sit in the dark on the floor feeling so afraid. It was utterly stupid. They couldn't do anything to her when there was a houseful of people upstairs.

She got to her feet, determined to march right past them.

But her hand hesitated on the doorknob. She didn't trust Deven and his friends. They'd do something stupid to make her react; humiliate her just for a laugh.

She couldn't face it. She really couldn't.

Jay backed away from the door, looking for a distraction to keep her from thinking about needing the loo. She crept back across the room, picked up her book, and tried to read. It was virtually impossible in the fading light, and straining to make out the words only made her head hurt more. She needed her light on, but the risk wasn't worth taking.

She always had a torch under her mattress in the flat above the grocer's, so she could read after her mum had gone to bed. Jay had read thousands of books like that in those few years. She always had to finish the page, or the chapter, or, occasionally, the whole book, before she could put it down. She hadn't thought about the torch since they'd moved, because she hadn't needed it. No one checked up on what time she went to sleep. She could have read all night if she had wanted to, and sometimes she did. She'd probably have to tonight.

The torch had to be in one of her suitcases or at the back of one of the drawers, although she couldn't remember packing it. She searched frantically until she remembered that her mum had stripped the bed and packed her lacy duvet for her. She probably hadn't even noticed the torch under the mattress. Jay cursed her luck and reluctantly placed the book back on the bedside table. She wasn't going to be reading tonight after all.

A glance at the clock told her that an hour had passed. Outside, the sky had darkened to a deep, inky blue. It would be pitch black soon. She climbed up on to her desk, hoping to catch a glimpse of her mum. Her windows faced out on to the corner of the garden and from that angle it was impossible to see if anyone was out on the main lawn. She stuck her head out further, wondering what any remaining guests would make of a fifteen-year-old girl wriggling out of a basement window.

She knew she couldn't squeeze through even if she tried – it was way too narrow. And getting stuck half in, half out of the window would be a total nightmare – especially if Auntyji spotted her. Auntyji had idled away untold hours of her life watching Bollywood films, and the scenario that would naturally spring to her suspicious mind would involve her shameless good-for-nothing niece wreaking disgrace and shame upon the family name by trying to sneak out to spend the night with her lover, or something equally daft.

Thinking about it, that wasn't such a bad idea. But not through the window. She was going to have to quite literally face the music if she wanted to get out of her room.

Jay stepped back from the window. She didn't notice the collection of pens and pencils strewn across her desk until it was too late. Her right foot slid across them and she went toppling backwards. She hit the floor with a resounding thump and a scream escaped her before she could suppress it. She lay in the dark, winded. It took her a few minutes to realize that she wasn't actually hurt, and that the music had stopped.

Had they heard her scream?

She thought it unlikely, but she should get into bed and pretend she was asleep, just in case. She thought about crawling under the bed and squeezing into the far corner by the wall, wedged safely behind the suitcases. But suddenly her bedroom door shot open and the room was flooded with a cold glare of artificial light.

Jay recoiled from it. She never used the main basement light – it was just a naked light bulb and it made the room look bleak and seedy.

Jay blinked, and blinked again, hoping those slightly scuffed large brown loafers weren't standing on the dull brown carpet tiles of her room. She knew who the shoes belonged to. She looked up apprehensively.

He was swaying in the doorway, his eyes little more than bleary, bloodshot slits. She heard the voices behind him. The voices of his friends. He was grinning that stupid lopsided smile of his.

She didn't smile back.

CHAPTER 10

Jay raised a hand to shield her eyes from the light, and struggled to her feet, wincing at the sudden pain in her hip. She was going to have a nasty bruise in the morning.

'Tripped over,' she said, by way of explanation. 'What do you want?'

'We heard noises. Thought someone was trying to break in,' he replied. He surveyed the room, taking in the obvious fact that she was very much alone. 'Didn't know you were in here all on your lonesome,' he said. His designer shirt was stained with curry, and his words were slurred.

'Yeah? Well, it is my room, you know!'

'OK, OK – don't get your knickers in a twist. Just

thought someone was trying to break in.'

More like wondering how to break out, Jay thought. 'As you can see, no one's breaking in. Surprised you can hear anything over that racket you're making.' He gave no sign of leaving. She was going to have to tell him to go. 'Shut the door on your way out, please,' she said, folding her arms in front of her. 'Some of us are trying to get some sleep.'

'Sleep! Get real, Jay,' he laughed. 'We can't let you sleep – not when there's a party going on. You're missing out on all the fun! Come and join us.' He pushed the door wide open in invitation. 'We know all about you, Jay, what kind of fun you really like.' He wagged his finger at her. 'You naughty, naughty girl. But we can show you some fun. More fun than you'll get with that *gora*.'

Jay wanted to die. He'd made her think it was OK – that he was cool about the 'white boy', about Matt. He'd said 'Your little secret is safe with me', and she'd trusted him. But he'd tricked her, lied to her, the devious shit. A knot of fear twisted inside Jay's stomach. How the hell was she going to get out of this?

Drunk people could be amusing. Her uncle had been hilarious this afternoon, stumbling and bumbling about. Deven and his mates were a different kind of drunk – and they weren't in the least bit funny.

Deven turned to his mates and said something that

Jay couldn't quite catch. They began to jeer and laugh and make grotesque, squelchy kissy-kissy noises in the background. She wanted to smack them all in the face and tell them to grow up, but that would have got their backs right up, and they were looking for any excuse to get rowdy. She was still hoping that they would get bored and leave her alone. And pigs might fly.

'No thanks. I'm too tired to dance,' she said. 'Like I said, I was trying to get to sleep, so if you don't mind turning it down a bit . . . Thanks.' She placed her hand decisively on the door, hoping he'd take the hint, but Deven stood his ground. She started to push the door back at him. He planted his foot against it.

'Come on, Jay, I know you're not one of those shy girls!' He leaned in, close to her face. 'You've been kissing boys.'

He was making out she was some kind of harlot, when she'd only ever kissed Matt, and that was only recently! 'Go away! You're drunk!' She pushed at the door, trying to shut it, trying to drive him out, but he refused to budge. She wasn't strong enough to push him out. A bubble of fear gurgled inside her. She inched back.

Deven reached out to stroke Jay's cheek, but she saw it coming and swatted his hand away. She glared up, her chin jutting out and eyes blazing with anger.

'What the hell are you doing, Deven? I said no! Get

out of my room right now! Get out!' Her words were tough, but there was a little tremor in her voice that betrayed her fear. It was a fatal sign of weakness, and it told him all he needed to know. She was frightened. Powerless. And he leaped on it.

She reached for the door again and pushed it against him, but he caught hold of her hand.

'Let go of me, you shithead!' But he wasn't listening.

'Not getting rid of me that easily, my little Jay,' he said, wagging his finger in her face. 'Tonight we're gonna have a dance.'

With a quick jerk, he'd yanked her out of her room. Fighting back wasn't going to work. Jay had to play along, play it cool, and look as though she didn't give a toss and that they didn't scare her. She would have that dance, but at some point she would find a way of making a run for the stairs.

The gym was unrecognizable. It reeked of stale sweat and alcohol. Cans of beer, and half-empty bottles of whiskey and rum were strewn all over the place. Dirty plates lay on every surface, and cigarettes spilled out of overflowing ashtrays. And Deven's mates were gawping at her as though they'd never seen a girl before. She shrank away from their hungry eyes.

The music was back on – some generic R&B bhangra mix; all the tracks sounded the same to her. Deven's mates crowded round in a circle, clapping in time to the beat as Deven flung her to and fro, swinging her round and round. Their moves bore only the vaguest resemblance to dancing, nothing like the dancers she had watched that afternoon, with their floating skirts and mesmerizing motion. There was nothing fluid about this – but then how could there be when Deven's feet were in the grip of Johnnie Walker's finest Red Label whiskey, while her feet just wanted to wing their way up the stairs to the safety of her mother's arms?

Time passed in a blur, and the flushed drunken faces of Deven and his mates seemed to merge with the hard-edged shiny chrome of the gym equipment. Round and round she went, caught on a demented merry-go-round. Her necklace caught on Deven's shirt button, but before she could do anything about it, he flung her away and it snapped. She screamed as her precious gold-heart locket, which her mum had retrieved from the pawnbroker, went flying through the air. She didn't see where it landed.

Jay couldn't take any more. She had to get out. But she couldn't run for it when he held her hand so tight. Before the next track started, she shouted, 'Deven! Stop! I've had enough!'

He laughed in her face.

'Stop, I said!'

He held on harder.

'You're hurting me! Please stop!'

He grinned inanely, but he didn't stop. He hurled her about as though she were a rag doll that would bend and twist whichever way he wanted. It felt as though her arm was being ripped out of its socket. She tried to break free, but his grip merely tightened. He wasn't letting go of her. She wanted to cry. Maybe that would stop him when all the screaming and shouting hadn't. She couldn't even aim a kick at where it would really hurt him, because half the time her feet didn't even touch the ground.

Then, suddenly, he released her and she went hurtling backwards. Her mouth opened in a silent scream, waiting for the inevitable crunch when she would smack into the wall. But she didn't hit the wall. One of his friends was waiting to catch her. He flipped her round before she could catch her breath and his face loomed into hers, his wet lips puckered. She screamed and ducked her head to the side to avoid him, but he found her neck and slobbered at it.

Jay struck upwards with her knee and connected with his groin. He cried out and raised his hand to strike her. She broke free and stumbled away, looking wildly around, trying to get her bearings.

She saw the corridor leading away from the gym to the stairs, but before she could move towards it, Deven grabbed her and pulled her back. She kicked him hard in the shins, but he didn't seem to feel it. Alcohol had desensitized him. She lashed out harder, twisting round in his grip to get a better aim, but the next kick went wide of its target as he drew her in close to his body. Still she fought. Her fingers pinched into his flesh.

But he simply grunted, his eyes hard, uncaring; he was enjoying the fight.

Any minute now someone would come down to the cellar. Her mum would come down. They hadn't seen each other all day. Nothing so terrible could happen here, with people upstairs. Deven and his crew were drunk but they weren't complete idiots.

Then she heard Deven say, 'She's mine first!'

She couldn't have heard him right; he couldn't have just said that. It wasn't possible. He wouldn't. They wouldn't. He must have been referring to the next dance, not to anything else because . . . because . . . Jay's eyes flicked across their faces, and five drunken men leered back at her.

Her heart plummeted deep into the pit of her stomach and she retched violently. Deven dragged her over to his friend and stabbed a chubby finger into his chest to make his point. She wanted to be sick, to cover him in her vomit.

Her legs buckled beneath her and she started to cry.

'Let me go,' she sobbed. Tears streamed down her face. 'Please! Please let me go!' The fear threatened to consume her.

But Deven was beyond hearing, beyond caring. 'Come on, Jay,' he whooped, dragging her up on to her feet. 'Now we'll have some real fun!' he shouted, and swung her round.

Her dad used to swing her round and round the garden when she was little. She used to love it. He would hold her firmly under her arms so she wouldn't slip out and fall tumbling on to the lawn and hurt herself. He swung her round and round and she would throw her head back, the clouds and the trees and the whole wide world spinning with her, laughing and giggling and shouting 'More, more!', and he would indulge her. When he set her down it was always so carefully, so tenderly. He would keep his arms about her, just in case she fell over dizzy. But before the world stopped spinning, she would jump up and down and shout 'Again, again, again, Daddy', until he relented. 'OK, Jaya, just one more time,' he'd respond. Afterwards they would fall in a heap on the soft grass, out of breath.

But Deven's arms were not her father's arms. They were wrapped around her so tight it hurt. She could barely breathe, but he pulled her tighter still, up hard against his body. With a damp, hot hand in her hair, he tilted her face towards his, his foul whiskey breath sour. She tried to pull away, but he swung her round and slammed her up against the wall, pinning her back like a specimen on display; his hands were crawling all over her, feeling her, touching her where no one had touched her before, where she did not want to be touched.

Jay's world was imploding.

She tasted bitter bile in her mouth and began to retch, but he would not stop. She screamed again and again, a hoarse shrieking that finally penetrated his drunken fog and surprised him.

It only stopped him momentarily, but the words were already formulated in her mouth and she screamed them again and again. 'Help! Help!'

As if in answer, the music stopped abruptly, mid-beat, and the room went quiet. Over Deven's shoulder, Jay saw Ash standing next to the stereo, the plug in his hands. He let it drop to the floor. Thank God for Ash. She wanted to throw her arms around him.

Quite calmly, he asked, 'What are you playing at, Deven?'

'Bugger off!'

'Mum sent me down. The neighbours are complaining. They can hear the music all the way down the road. She told me to pull the plug.'

Deven's head snapped round, his eyes narrowed with rage. 'You stupid bloody idiot! You've wrecked the CD in there! It was rare. Paid a fortune for it!' he growled. 'Mum didn't say anything. She wouldn't dare. Piss off! Now!'

Ash did not move. 'Go and ask her yourself, if you don't believe me. She wants everyone out.'

'You get out!' Deven bellowed.

'No.'

Jay could feel the anger and the rage through the hands that held her pinned to the wall. He'd lost control, driven crazy by alcohol. She was afraid for Ash and for herself. Deven let go of her and lurched across the room. 'You liar!' he spat in his brother's face. 'If she really wants us out, she can damn well come down and tell me herself.'

Ash stood his ground. 'She wants them out – now,' he said coldly.

Released from his grip, Jay's legs gave way and she slid down the wall. She wrapped her arms around her body, holding herself together while she waited for Deven to make his next move. She couldn't get up yet; she was shaking too hard and couldn't feel her legs.

Deven's hands had clenched into fists and he raised one towards his brother. Instantly one of his friends was at his side, pulling him away. 'Come on, Dev. That's your bro. Leave it. It's not worth it. Let's go. I know a good place. Get all the fun you want there, you know? Come on, man.'

Deven shrugged his friend off and turned back to Ash. How long would Ash stand and face his brother's intimidation before deciding to get the hell out? She had to move; she had to be ready. Jay struggled to her feet, ignoring her quivering legs.

Ash hadn't moved, but a small muscle at the corner of his eye had begun to flicker.

'I told you to get the hell out, you little prick. So what're you still doing here, huh?' Deven demanded. His face was inches from his brother's, but still Ash didn't flinch.

'Following orders. Mum's orders,' Ash replied.

Without warning, Deven's hand shot out and thumped Ash squarely in the middle of his chest, sending him stumbling backwards. He stepped in towards him again. 'Something wrong with your ears? I said get the hell out.' Another thump landed on Ash's chest.

Ash caught hold of Deven's hand before it struck him again. 'There's nothing wrong with *my* ears. The neighbours are about to call the police. Don't think that would be a good idea, would it? Coppers down here, breaking up your party. They might find something' – Ash looked pointedly at the ashtrays and then back to his brother, his mouth tightening in a hard line – '. . . incriminating.' He released Deven's hand.

'Don't think you've got away with pulling this shit,' Deven hissed, spraying spittle into Ash's face. Ash wiped it off with his sleeve. 'I'll sort you out later, little bro. Teach you a thing or two,' he added. 'Like when you were a kid.'

'Yeah? I'm terrified,' Ash retorted.

'I remember you used to be scared, all right!' Deven's mouth twisted into a snarl as he laughed. 'Go on – run and squeal to Mum about me, like you used to. She never believed you then. She won't believe you now.'

Ash shook his head. 'You'll never change, will you? Still as thick as you ever were. Just get out. All of you. Or you know what? I'll call the police myself.'

Deven drew his fist back. There was murder in his eyes. Jay cringed. Everything had spiralled out of control. She didn't want Ash to get pulverized by his brother. They were both about the same height, but Ash was skin and bone compared to Deven's brawn, and he didn't have his brother's mean streak.

Jay held her breath as Deven's fist sliced through the air towards Ash. Ash ducked quickly, but Deven dropped his fist at the last minute and laughed. He'd made his brother look foolish. Now, at last, he was ready to go. He jerked his head at his mates to get their stuff. One by one, they stumbled out. Deven was the last to leave.

Jay watched him lumbering out of the gym. Relief flooded through her. She slumped against the handrails of the treadmill, every bone in her body hurting.

But then he stopped and looked back, raising his finger and pointing it directly at her. She pressed herself back against the handrail, cowering under his venomous glare.

'I'll come back for you too,' he hissed.

She shuddered, even though she knew it was an idle threat. Deven couldn't get her now. He'd be out partying all night, tormenting someone else, and he would probably end up crashing at one of his mates', too drunk to find his way home. Tomorrow he would be gone, back to uni, and the next time he came back to visit his family, she wouldn't be living in this hellhole.

She was going to tell her mum they had to leave. She'd make her mum understand.

She'd make her listen, this time.

CHAPTER 11

'You OK?' Ash asked.

Jay nodded, not trusting her voice yet. She was still shaking.

'Are you sure, Jay?'

She cleared her throat. 'Yeah, I think so.' But she wasn't at all sure what would happen if she let go of the handrail that was holding her up. She held on to it tight.

'You don't have to worry about them – they won't be back. Well, not tonight anyway.' Ash took in the room and shook his head. 'Bloody hell! Some party they were having down here.' He started picking up cans of beer off the floor and placing them on the bench. 'This gear cost a fortune. I can't believe he let them trash it like this. Everything's a mess. There's beer and stuff,' he pulled a disgusted face at the remnants of a kebab perched on top of the cross trainer, 'everywhere.'

Jay couldn't care less about the state of the gym. She was trembling, she hurt all over and she wanted to curl up in her bed and cry. But not in front of Ash. She needed to ask him something before he left. 'Do me a favour, Ash?'

'Yeah?'

'Can you fix a bolt on my door for me?'

'What, now?'

She was so tempted to say 'Yes, do it now', but she didn't. Ash looked shattered. It was late and Deven had gone. 'No, tomorrow'll be fine.'

'Yeah, sure. I'll see what we have in the garage. Otherwise I'll nip out and pick one up from the hardware store.'

'Thanks.'

'No problem.' He turned to leave. 'Jay? Look, I'm sorry about what happened tonight. Deven's always been like that. He's a nasty piece of work.'

'It's OK, Ash.'

'No, it's not OK. Luckily he doesn't come back too often any more.'

She thought he was going to hug her for a second, but in the end he just gave her arm a quick pat.

He took his glasses off and polished them on his

T-shirt. 'Listen, I can do the bolt for you now.'

Jay was tempted, but in the end she shook her head. She wanted to be on her own. 'It's OK. It's late.'

'Then I'll do it first thing in the morning. OK?'

'Thanks, Ash.'

'Can I get you anything to eat before I go?'

She'd only grabbed a couple of samosas at lunch, but food was the last thing she wanted. 'No. I'm all right. Is my mum still up?'

'She went to bed. She asked me to make sure you were OK – with all the noise going on down here, you know. That's why I came down.'

Why hadn't she come down herself? Jay wondered. She knew the answer. And it didn't make her feel any better. 'You told Deven your mum sent you down.'

'She didn't – but, trust me, she'll be very happy they've gone. She never liked Deven's old friends much. She thinks they're a bad influence on him. If you ask me, he's the one who's a bad influence. I had to make up that bit about calling the police. It was the only way to get rid of them.'

'It was . . . scary for a while.' Jay's voice was wobbling again, but she didn't want to break down in front of Ash.

'Are you sure you're OK?'

'I'll be fine now.' She gave him a brave half-smile to reassure him.

* * *

As soon as he'd gone, Jay shut her door on the gym and tried to blank out everything that had happened, but the tears were already falling, and this time she let them. She hated Deven, hated this house, hated her mum, hated her life.

Exhaustion seeped out of every pore in her body, but she couldn't go to bed without washing off the traces their grasping hands and slobbering mouths had left on her. She picked her way carefully back through the debris of the gym, and locked the bathroom door. She was in half a mind to get her duvet and sleep in there, where she could lock herself away from Deven. But there was nothing to be afraid of now that he'd gone.

Upstairs, everyone was fast asleep. The house was silent but for the ticking of her clock. Once she was clean, Jay climbed into bed and snuggled under the covers, closing her eyes and expecting to fall asleep straight away – but sleep eluded her.

An idea occurred to her as she lay in the dark. A mad, wild idea. She switched the light on and sat up. Matt's house wasn't far. She could get there in less than ten minutes if she ran. His mum wouldn't mind her turning up on the doorstep in the middle of the night – not if it was an emergency, which it was, of sorts.

Could she leave in the middle of the night, without

telling her mum? No. But she couldn't wake her mum up at this time of night either. Neela would tell her off for making a silly fuss over nothing. And the most painful thing of all was that her mum probably wouldn't believe her if she told her how they'd treated her. Even Jay could barely believe it.

What would have happened if Ash hadn't walked in when he did?

Fresh tears sprang to her eyes and her body heaved as sobs tore through her. Tomorrow she would force her mum to listen – and she wouldn't spare her any details.

Surely Mum would have to do something about it then?

Jay took her phone out of her bag and saw four missed calls – all from Matt. She'd fallen asleep after leaving that text on his phone, and had slept through his return calls. And then all that shit with Deven and his mates had happened. She rang Matt, but his phone was off and she couldn't just turn up on his doorstep without warning. After sending him a text confirming their arrangement to meet in the park in the morning, she took two painkillers, and set her alarm for eight. There was no way she was going to spend a minute longer in the house than was absolutely necessary. She'd sit and read a book in the park until Matt showed up.

Jay felt less anxious now, but still couldn't sleep,

so she picked *Tess of the d'Urbervilles* up and started reading. Matt was right: it was all doom and gloom. Happy endings were for fairy tales, and *Tess* was no fairy tale.

It was almost three in the morning when her eyelids finally began to droop. With a last glance at her door to make sure it was firmly shut, Jay switched off her light.

The strange dreams began immediately. She was in a version of Hardy's rural England – rolling farmland, but not quite. There was something different, but she couldn't put her finger on what it was. Far off in the distance, stone farmhouses dotted the horizon and small figures moved about. Some kind of festival was taking place. She heard the faint sounds of laughter and gaiety. No one was working.

Jay was alone, surrounded by vast fields of crops. Huge threshing machines stood idle across the field. There was so much work to be done and she could not do it alone. She called out to the people in the distance. She called and called but they could not hear her. They were too far away. Above, the sun blazed with unrelenting intensity. Her mouth was parched and dry; her lips were cracked, like the scorched ground beneath her feet. She was burning up. She had to find water. She began walking towards the horizon, towards the farmhouses and the distant dots that she knew were people. She would find water there, and they would help her. And then she stopped.

She heard a creaking. She turned around but there was nothing there, only the threshing machines, standing as tall as giants among the sheaves of wheat. It was the breeze that made the threshing machines creak, she decided. She resumed her walk. There was a long way to go, as the farmhouses were perched on top of the hills and she was in the valley. Again, she heard the same sound. It could not have been the breeze that caused the machines to creak, for there was not even the slightest stirring of air. She could not bring herself to face the threshing machines until the idea came to her that the heat of the sun could cause the machines to creak. Still, her heart was beating fast and she did not know why.

She glanced back briefly. Were they closer? No, surely that was impossible. She was suffering the ill effects of the searing sun, and unless she reached water soon, her hallucinations would only worsen. Jay quickened her pace. She did not remember how she came to be out here on her own, when the rest of the world was somewhere else.

More creaking and scraping split the silence and she clapped her hands over her ears. If she did not hear it and did not see it, then it could not be happening. But the sounds grew louder and louder until they filled the air around her and she could no longer ignore them. She had to see what was coming behind her.

She forced herself to stop, and with a fleeting backward glimpse she saw that there were three of them, moving so slowly you could barely detect their movement. She turned back and looked ahead towards the distant people. They could not help her.

Unable to help herself, she watched, mesmerized, as they limbered up. Their heads rotated from side to side; looking, seeking. With mounting horror, she realized the machines were looking for her. Jay began to run and the three figures caught sight of her movement. In unison, they stepped forward. They were coming for her.

She headed for the horizon at full speed, through endless sun-kissed fields of golden wheat. But the machines moved faster – and something else was happening too. They were mutating. Their metal bodywork was transforming into grotesque bodies, and their arms snapped at her fleeing back. Her screams were deafened by their thunderous roaring. They tore up the fields, gouging deep black scars into the ground as they churned up the earth below. She felt the rumbling and the ground tearing beneath her feet, yet on and on she ran, without a backward glance. But the roaring was closing in on her.

Her hair came loose in the wind and flew like a

mane behind her. But her feet were as light as puffs of air, and bore her swiftly across the fields. The horizon seemed just as far off, but that did not matter because she was getting away. She was too fast for the lumbering machines. She would be free soon.

Then suddenly, silence. She had outrun them. She was safe. She slowed to a stop, catching her breath, and turned around. Jay was not alone.

There was one machine left, the biggest and strongest of them all, and it made no sound as it came for her.

Silent and deadly.

She knew it would hurt her if she did not get away. She had to run, faster than before, but terror made her clumsy. It made her stumble. The sun disappeared and the sky suddenly darkened to night. Jay could no longer see where she was going or what lay in her path. Time and time again she stumbled. Her long dress sent her tripping and tumbling over bundled sheaves of wheat, ripping and tearing as it caught in her feet. Her hair was plastered to her face with sweat and tears and she pushed it away so she could see. But it was too dark. She scrambled backwards – whimpering, trying to find her feet, trying to escape – but it was too late.

The machine had reached Jay and was upon her in an instant, its arms wide open to embrace her within its unforgiving clutches. She screamed, but its hand whipped her coldly across the face, the hard metal slashing through her soft flesh. She tasted salty blood from her cut lip. The other hand struck a blow across her right eye, blinding her.

She could not see. She could not speak. Tears rolled down her face and mingled with her blood, salt cutting sharp as a knife into her lacerated lip. It hurt. She screamed again, but it covered her mouth, silencing her. But this could not be real. This was a nightmare. This was not really happening to her. She was asleep. It was not real. So why then could she taste blood? Why did it hurt?

And why could she not wake up?

Jay kicked out, but her legs would not move. They were trapped beneath its bulk, and it weighed down heavily upon her. She struck out with her hands, her palms closing to form tightly clenched fists. She punched and pummelled harder and faster, but it was far stronger than her. She would not give in, even as her nails drew pearls of blood from her palms. Still she lashed out with all her might, screaming, *No! No! No!*

But it would not stop. And the people in the distance were no longer there. No one heard her cries.

It kept her pinned beneath it, squeezing the breath out of her body. She rasped for air; her lungs screaming for help. She twisted and turned, searching for a weak point where she could hurt it – throw it off her, and run for help. But it took one of her arms and trapped it, while it ripped and tore at her clothes, shredding them from her body – leaving her exposed, naked to its eyes. Its mouth opened in a leer, saliva dribbling from one corner in anticipation.

She sobbed.

Please.

Please.

Stop.

Help me, someone.

Mummy, help me . . .

Stop. Stop. Stop.

But it would not stop. Not until it had finished.

It grunted as it rolled off her. She could see through one eye, see its face. But she did not want to see. She clamped it shut quickly. Too late. Too late.

She had seen its face, *his* face. The face of evil. It would be forever etched in her mind.

Nothing would ever be the same again.

PART TWO

After.

CHAPTER 12

How far she had gone she didn't know, but she could not stop, not yet. She couldn't stay here sitting on someone's garden wall – not when they were in their driveway whispering and wondering who she was, what she was doing.

The thought that they might take her for a druggie made her stop rocking. The fear that they might call the police made her push off the wall and start walking again, even though her legs, her whole body, screamed with exhaustion. Jay was so tired. All she wanted to do was to sit down for a while and not move, but it was a hot, sunny Sunday afternoon, and everyone seemed to have picked that day to tend their front gardens. There were people everywhere. Happy people, normal people, doing everyday things. Did they see her as she stumbled past them? Did they point at her and whisper among themselves – *What do you think's wrong with her?*

Jay staggered into a deserted bus shelter and sat down, just as her legs were giving up. Sobs tore through her and broke free. She hunched over, cradling herself, as people walked by. After a long while she got up and started walking again, her eyes fixed on her feet as they followed the pavement.

She should not think, not about anything. She had to concentrate on one thing and that was walking. She had to get much further away, as far away as possible. She had to get to where no one knew her.

At a crossroad, her step faltered. The intersection was busy with cars. She turned left, anxious to get away from the noise of the traffic; it made her head throb. Set back off the road was a small building, an old red-brick two-storey building with a car park in front of it. The word *Library* was etched into the arch above the entrance. It made her gasp as she recognized it. She must be mistaken. Jay glanced round wildly, searching for a road sign, and saw other things that were familiar: a parade of shops, a row of offices, a small park.

She was in Northwood – miles and miles away from No.42.

Had she really walked that far?

She raced past the library, hoping no one would see her, recognize her from the old days. They had lived less than ten minutes' drive away from here. Her old school, St Montague's, was up the hill. Her old friends lived all around the area. But how would they recognize her, when she couldn't even recognize herself?

Tears blinded her as she reeled from the memories of those days of innocence, those days of living life without care. Jay couldn't let her old friends see how far she had fallen, so she ran and ran until exhaustion slowed her pace.

She walked head down – blindly stumbling, not thinking – straight into a woman.

'Sorry, sorry,' she mumbled, instantly bending down to retrieve the contents of the woman's shopping bag. She didn't look at the woman's face, she couldn't bear to meet her eyes. There wasn't much shopping to pick up – some fruit and vegetables, a tin of tomatoes, a packet of paneer and frozen peas, a loaf of brown bread and a pint of milk. The woman was Asian, Jay suddenly realized. She handed the bag back to the woman with another garbled apology, stepping quickly away.

Jay's head was all mixed up, but somehow she could list every item in the bag as though they had gone past her at the checkout in the supermarket where she worked.

'Are you all right, my dear?' There was a faint

trace of an Indian accent in the woman's voice, but her English had a cultured, more sophisticated tone. Nothing like Aunty V's broad, Punjabi English. Still, Jay knew she had to get away.

The woman reached forward and touched Jay's arm lightly. The tender touch jolted Jay. Its kindness made her tremble. It made her chest tighten with unbroken sobs. It made her head swim with images she wanted to obliterate, images of a face she wanted to destroy.

It made her want to say *Please help me, please . . .*

Tears welled afresh in her eyes. She stumbled back a step. She could not, would not accept help from an Asian woman. Not after her mother had let her down. Not after being treated like a skivvy by Aunty V.

Jay opened her mouth to speak, and felt a sharp sting in her lip as the cut reopened. She licked the little pearls of blood at the corner of her mouth and wiped the tears away with her sleeve, brushing across her badly bruised eye, making it throb violently. It had almost completely closed over and she could barely see through it.

What had the nice lady asked her? *Are you all right, my dear?*

She nodded mutely, not trusting herself to speak, as another sob rose in her throat.

'You should go home and put some ice on your eye or you will not be able to see out of it by tomorrow.'

Go home. Go home. The words repeated themselves in Jay's head. Yes, she should go home. But where do you go when you don't have a home you want to go to? Where should she go? What should she do?

If she told the lady that she had nowhere to go, would she let her go home with her? Would she sit her down in her cosy kitchen and give her a packet of frozen peas for her eye, while she made them both a nice cup of tea to make everything all better again? Would she make all the pain go away?

'I can't go home. I'm running away,' Jay blurted without thinking.

The woman stepped closer and looked at her more carefully. Jay could tell she wasn't sure how to respond, which didn't surprise her. All the lady had done was to ask if she was all right and Jay had landed a bombshell on her. She expected the woman to tell her she must go home, that running away from problems wasn't the solution, that her family would be worried sick about her, but she didn't say any of those things.

Instead, she said, 'Jay? Is that you?'

Jay looked up at the woman's face for the first time, and the shock of recognition made her draw her breath in sharply. The short grey hair, the dark brows, the mole just above the woman's lip, which looked like a beauty spot . . . She'd last seen her at the temple on her dad's anniversary. She remembered, with a pang, hiding from her – because it dredged up memories of when her dad was alive, of when she was at school at St Montague's.

'It *is* you. Do you remember me? I am matron. Well, I am plain old Sita Anandhati now.'

Jay stumbled further away. She didn't want to be recognized. She didn't want anyone who knew her to see her like this – and especially not her old school matron, Mrs Anandhati. 'No. You've got the wrong person.' She hurried away, but the woman followed her.

'Stop. Please, stop,' she called after Jay.

Jay marched on, tears running down her face. Mrs Anandhati was the last person she'd expected to bump into. All the girls in her old school had loved Mrs Anandhati – she never let you bunk off classes to lie in the sick room without a good reason, but she always had time for you, and a kind word.

So what if the matron at her old school had recognized her? She didn't know where Jay lived now. She didn't know *this* Jay.

Jay didn't get far. Her marching had slowed to a walk. She was shattered: her legs ached, her eye was throbbing. And deep inside her, there was an unbearable pain.

She didn't know where she was going anyway. Nothing mattered any more. She tripped on a loose paving stone and a hand reached out and caught hold of her arm, steadying her. The hand remained on her arm; Jay didn't have the strength to shrug it off. She turned to face her old matron.

'I live just down the road. Come and have a cup of tea with me.'

'Tea?' Jay mumbled weakly.

'Yes, a cup of tea.' Jay could see that Mrs Anandhati was trying not to stare at her bad eye, but her eyes kept flitting towards it. It must have looked grotesque. 'Please come with me, Jay.'

The offer was desperately tempting. It would get dark soon – what would she do then? All alone and lost in a city full of millions of people. Where would she hide: a park, or a doorway, or a subway? She had seen runaways and homeless people camping out in places like that, wrapped in grubby layers of rags or cardboard boxes. She might be all right sleeping rough tonight – it was warm enough, and maybe by tomorrow, if she could get her brain to work by then, she would decide what to do next, or find a better hiding place. She would be all right. Hundreds of kids did this.

But Mrs Anandhati's offer was tempting. She could put off sleeping rough for a while, go and sit in her old matron's house while she figured out what to do next. But this woman didn't really want her in her house. She was just being kind because she knew Jay once, in a different lifetime.

The jumble of thoughts made Jay's head hurt. She didn't know what to do.

In the end, she shook her head. No one could help her. She just wanted to curl up somewhere, fall asleep and never have to wake up.

Mrs Anandhati seemed not to notice because she said, 'Come along,' in that brisk no-nonsense voice Jay remembered from school. 'I'll get that eye sorted out for you as well. Come on, it's not far. Just down the road.'

Jay was taken firmly by the arm and steered back down the street. She tried demurring again, but Mrs Anandhati paid no attention to her. They had only walked a few hundred yards when she stopped and pushed open a garden gate.

'Here we are,' she said. 'I told you it wasn't far.'

She led Jay up a stone-paved path, through a neat garden, to a pillar-box red front door flanked with pots bursting with early summer blooms. The house was a whitewashed semi with ivy framing the front door and creeping round the windows, but the tall hedges on either side of the house and at the front kept it private from its neighbours.

Mrs Anandhati took a clutch of keys out of her handbag. She unlocked the front door and pushed it wide open.

'Go straight through to the kitchen and sit down,'

she instructed, 'and I'll put the kettle on.'

Jay walked through the hallway, immediately struck by how different the house felt to No.42. She took a deep breath and let it out. If it had felt like No.42, she knew she would have turned around and run as far as she could.

In the kitchen, Mrs Anandhati handed Jay an ice pack wrapped inside a tea towel. 'Hold this up against your eye firmly. It might still help with the swelling.'

Jay watched her old matron making tea and unpacking the shopping bag, while she sat silently, the ice pack pressed lightly against her eye. Mrs Anandhati was tall and slim, and her neck was long, almost swanlike. Her grey hair was cropped short, but it suited her angular face.

The clock on the kitchen wall said half past four, which meant she had been walking for over four hours. But it still didn't feel as though she had put enough distance between herself and No.42. For the time it took for a kettle to boil and a cup of tea to be drunk, she was safe – and grateful for the brief respite Sita Anandhati had offered.

The older woman set a cup of sweet, weak tea in front of Jay, and a plate of biscuits, and two painkillers. She took the ice pack out of Jay's hand and touched the bruised area around her eye gently. Her touch was feather-light, but Jay flinched instinctively.

'I'm not going to hurt you,' she said. 'I need to make sure the cut isn't deep.' She examined it carefully. 'No – no stitches, but I am afraid the ice will not do the trick by itself. If you had iced it at the time it might have helped, but I'm guessing this is a day old or thereabouts. Keep the ice on it for now. Have you eaten anything today, Jay?'

Jay had a vague recollection of eating some lunch the day before. But she didn't feel hungry at all.

'Well, have a biscuit with your tea and then take the pills. They will take the edge off the pain. I'll heat up some soup for you in a while. How old are you now, Jay?'

Her birthday had only been a month ago. 'Fifteen.'

Sita nodded. She took Jay's hands in hers, noting the dark bruises around her wrists, the grazed knuckles, and turned them over. The crimson crescents sat out proudly in her palms. Sita opened a tube of antiseptic cream and rubbed it into Jay's palms and on to her knuckles where the skin had torn. She dabbed it on all the other scrapes and scratches she could see. 'These will heal up in no time,' she said reassuringly. She smiled at her.

Jay remembered that smile. Matron had always been kind. But this smile was full of sadness, and Jay could understand why. The last time matron had seen her, she had been a happy, outgoing girl. How was it possible that so much could change in three years?

Jay attempted to smile back, but instead her lips trembled violently and tears sprang to her eyes. She turned away quickly as they spilled down her cheeks, but matron had already seen them. The older woman stroked Jay's arms lightly, so she didn't hurt her, as silent sobs shuddered through the girl in front of her.

'It's all right, Jay. It's all right,' she murmured. 'You're safe here. But please tell me, Jay, do you have any other injuries or pains anywhere?' Her light brown eyes looked searchingly into Jay's for an answer. She continued stroking Jay's arms until the shuddering subsided. Jay did not mind her touch; it was soothing, comforting.

Any other injuries? Any other pains? Jay couldn't tell her. Not about *that*. Not about what had happened. She couldn't say it, not ever. 'No, there's nothing more,' she whispered. 'Nothing.'

'Is there anyone you would like me to call?'

Jay shook her head emphatically. An image of her mum flashed through her mind, and another of Matt, but she couldn't let them see her, not with this shame written all over her face. 'No. Nobody.'

'Jay, you may not realize it, but you are in terrible shock.'

Jay stared at the tablecloth. It was brilliant white, embroidered with little daisies and buttercups, and with crocheted edges. How long could she make the tea last? How long before matron asked her to leave?

'And you're dead on your feet, too.' She seemed to come to a decision then. 'You need to sleep, and then we will see you how you feel. While you finish your tea, I will make up a bed for you. Don't worry if you cannot sleep, a little rest will be good. We will talk more later. All right, Jay?'

Jay thought she must be dreaming. 'I – I should go. I – I don't want to be any trouble.'

'You are no trouble, Jay. No trouble at all.'

'But –'

'No buts,' Mrs Anandhati said firmly. 'You told me you were running away. Where were you running away to? Who were you looking for? Where were you going?'

Jay didn't have any answers. People just ran away, didn't they? London was full of runaways, and they were always running *away* from something, never to . . .

'You see, you do not know. You must rest, and then we will talk and see what we can do. Do not be afraid, Jay. I will help you.'

Jay was suddenly seized by the fear that Mrs Anandhati might call them as soon as she was asleep. What if she knew where she lived now? She might call them to take her home. Or she might call the police and tell them that she had a runaway for them to deal with. 'You won't – you won't tell them I'm here, will you? Please don't! I'm not going back,' she cried in panic. 'Please,' she begged, 'please don't tell anyone I'm here.'

'Calm down, Jay. I promise I will not tell anybody. Anyway, who would I tell? I'm not going to call the police unless you want me to, and I do not have your family's phone number, do I? So I cannot call them. Although very soon your mother will be going out of her head with worry. Did you leave a note for her?'

A note? The thought hadn't even crossed Jay's mind. What would she have written? 'No. I . . . There wasn't time – I didn't think . . .'

'Never mind. She is bound to worry regardless. It is clear that you are running away from whoever did this to you at home, so I am not going to pick up the phone and send you right back to them.' She saw the uncertainty on Jay's face and added, 'I promise that you can trust me. I live alone, Jay, and I am trusting *you* here in my home. We must trust each other.'

Why? Jay wanted to ask, *Why are you helping me?* But she didn't have the energy. 'Thank you,' she whispered.

'You do not need to thank me, Jay. Please, finish your tea and take those pills. I will be back in a moment.'

Jay dutifully sipped at her tea, but couldn't stomach a biscuit. She took the tablets and sighed heavily into the silence. The ticking of the clock was soothing, and gradually her shoulders drooped as exhaustion overcame her. She was safe – for now.

By the time she put the cup down she was almost slumped over the table, oblivious to her surroundings. But then the creak of the kitchen door startled her and made her jump with a small cry. Her hand shot out and knocked over the tea cup, spilling the remains on the spotless tablecloth. It took her a moment to realize where she was and that the person standing in the doorway wasn't going to hurt her.

'I'm sorry! I'm so sorry!' she cried, looking from matron to the rapidly spreading brown stain. She grabbed the sponge from the sink and dabbed at the stains. 'I've ruined your tablecloth. I didn't hear you coming down the stairs. I'm such an idiot. I'm so –'

Mrs Anandhati placed her hand on Jay's shoulder. 'It is only a drop of tea.' She removed the sponge from Jay's hand and put it on the sink. 'It is easily washed out. Come with me.' She guided her out of the kitchen and through the hallway.

Jay stopped at the bottom stair. 'Matron?'

'Jay, you must call me Sita. We're not at St Montague's now.'

To Jay it sounded all wrong to address an older Indian woman by her first name. 'Um, Sitaji, are you –'

Sita raised her hand, stopping Jay mid-sentence. 'I may be older than you, Jay, but I would much rather you just call me Sita. In my family we only used those little extra terms of respect for the grandparents.' She smiled. 'My family in Kenya were never much into the old traditional ways. So please call me Sita.'

Jay nodded, relieved. 'Um, Sita, are you sure this is no trouble?'

'Oh, I am quite sure.' Sita fixed her with her brown eyes and raised her eyebrows. 'That is, unless you have somewhere else you would rather go? I could take you there if that is what you want.'

'No, no. There isn't anywhere else.'

'Then follow me,' she replied, and she continued up the stairs.

Jay took her trainers off and followed her up the carpeted stairs. At Aunty V's, there were pictures of Hindu gods and goddesses everywhere. Here, there were only family photographs lining the soft green walls, and at the top, the stairs opened out on to a large airy landing lit by a square window of stained glass. Against the rail at the top of the stairs was a side table with more family photographs vying for space on the narrow surface. A boy and a girl were sitting in a jeep, waving. It looked like they were on safari in Africa. Jay caught a glimpse of a much younger Sita with the two children on a beach, everyone smiling.

'My children,' Sita said. 'A long, long time ago.'

'It's a lovely photograph.'

'Yes, yes it is.' She sounded wistful, a faraway look in her eyes.

And not for the first time since she had entered Sita Anandhati's house, Jay wondered whether she had actually died last night and gone to heaven. Was that why she felt so comfortable with this woman? So comfortable that she was about to go and sleep in her house?

No. Jay knew why. Sita wasn't one of the Indian 'friends' her parents had known and socialized with, who had dropped them in double-quick time after her dad died and they lost all their money. And she didn't have anything to do with Aunty Vimala and her petty friends. It was simply because Sita Anandhati had been her old matron – a comforting and familiar face from a time when Jay had been the happiest girl in town.

CHAPTER 13

'This is my room.' Sita indicated a closed door to the left of the bookcase. 'And that's just an airing cupboard. There are extra towels in there if you need them. This is the bathroom. There's plenty of hot water if you wish to take a bath.' She carried on past it to another door. 'And this is where you can rest. I hope you will find it comfortable.'

Jay hesitated at the door.

'Come, Jay. There is no need to be shy.' Sita beckoned her with an outstretched hand.

It was a girl's room, pink and pretty, and simply the most perfect room she had ever seen.

'I really *have* died and gone to heaven,' she murmured softly. It couldn't be a dream, because everything looked too real. Maybe she had gone mad and completely lost her mind, or maybe she was lost *in* her mind. Had a strange survival instinct cast Jay's mind adrift from reality and carried her to a safe place, a place where she could hide for ever, where no one would find her?

The walls were covered with a thick creamy paper with raised pink roses dancing merrily across it. There was a matching pretty pink border running along the top of the walls. The furniture was made of solid wood and painted creamy-white, with pink and silver knobs on all the drawers and doors of the fitted wardrobe. There was a little vanity table with an oval mirror, a desk against the window with a view over a rambling garden. Two bookcases flanked the window. A small double bed, freshly made up with two fluffy towels folded neatly and placed at the end, completed the perfect little girl's bedroom. If only Jay could go back in time and be a little girl again.

Jay felt she could live in this room for ever and never have to come out – never want to come out. How she wished it was hers.

'It was my daughter's room,' Sita explained. 'Amala's room – although my granddaughter sleeps here now when they come to stay. But if you don't feel comfortable in here, I can always make up a bed for you in the other room.'

'No, no, it's not that. It's just that it's . . . too nice. Too perfect.'

Sita shooed Jay inside with the words, 'Please, make yourself at home. I will be downstairs or in the garden if you need me. Sleep for as long as you want. No one will disturb you.' And she shut the door, leaving Jay alone.

Jay perched gingerly on the edge of the bed, still wondering whether she had gone mad. Could she have summoned up someone from her past, someone like Sita, with just the power of her imagination?

If she was really here, then her mum was still there. In *that* house. Was she sick with worry? Probably. Why didn't that bother Jay? She didn't know the answer. The mere act of thinking was too tiring. The painkillers had kicked in, dulling some of the pain. But inside, she still hurt. She would always hurt.

Jay swung her legs on to the bed and lay down on top of the soft patchwork quilt – fully dressed, with the cap still on her head – and within seconds, a deep, dreamless sleep encased her like a tomb.

The room was dark when she woke up. Disorientated and suddenly scared, she bolted upright, sensing a presence at the door. Someone was there. Her heart skipped a beat and she panicked. She was ready to jump off the bed and hide – under the bed, or maybe in the back of the wardrobe, behind all the clothes.

Jay listened carefully, but there was no sound, no breathing other than her own ragged breath. She was completely alone. There was no one standing outside the room – no voices, no music, nothing at all – and she knew she wasn't there, in that terrible place. She was somewhere else, somewhere safe.

It was still light outside, but the curtains were drawn and a small night light plugged into the socket near the door cast a soft glow round the room. She shrugged off the blanket Sita must have covered her with while she slept, and took a long drink of water from the glass on the nightstand. Her cap was lying beside it. Her hands flew to her head as, with a start, she remembered that she'd hacked off all her hair. She ran her fingers through what was left of it, her fingers stopping before they reached her jaw-line. It was short. She wondered how bad it looked.

Jay got off the bed, her legs like jelly. The painkillers were wearing off. She walked across the room to the vanity table and sat down in front of it, but she was suddenly too afraid to look at her own reflection. What would it tell her?

She resisted the pull of the mirror and looked down instead, at the surface of the vanity table. There was a collection of hair clips and slides and hair bands that a little girl would use. On the left, a photograph of a young girl with long dark hair and big brown eyes beamed at her. She looked about eight or nine. She must be Sita's granddaughter, Jay thought. Finally, reluctantly, Jay's eyes travelled upwards, towards the mirror, and met those of the girl looking back.

It was the same girl she had seen this morning. The one she didn't recognize. The one she didn't like. She didn't want to look at her.

Jay stood up, trying to get away from the mirror, and winced as a sudden pain shot up deep from within the pit of her stomach, and from further below. It felt like her insides were tearing apart. The pain was excruciating. It made her legs tremble violently and she had to grasp hold of the back of the chair until the spasms passed. When they had gone, she found herself crouching on the floor on her knees, her head hanging down. She would not let herself think about the pain, about why it was there. She raised herself off the carpet and moved very slowly round the room.

She trailed her fingers lightly across the surface of the desk, opened the wardrobe doors a crack and peered in at the mixture of clothes that belonged to Sita's daughter and granddaughter. Stacks of old school books were piled up in another wardrobe. Jay picked one up. On the front it said: *Amala Anandhati, History, Year 8A.* Sita had kept all Amala's old school books. Jay wondered whether her own mum would have done the same, if things had turned out differently.

But they hadn't. They could never go back to the way they once were, to before they had moved into that house. They would have to go back years, to before her dad died, for a chance, a vague hope, that things might have turned out differently.

She slammed the door on those thoughts, refusing to let any memories drag her back to the abyss of the night before.

Jay switched the bedside light on, and kneeled down to take a closer look at the contents of the bookshelves. There was a huge mixture, from picture books to the complete series of *Malory Towers* books, which Jay had always wanted to read, and a shelf of classics, which immediately took Jay back to her childhood. Her dad had bought her a collection of beautifully bound collectors' editions. That was when they were still rich. She'd read them all, loved them and treasured them: *Little Women*, *Black Beauty*, *The Secret Garden*, *The Chronicles of Narnia*, *Ballet Shoes*.

Something inside her broke. Hot tears of self pity, anger and grief spilled out as she huddled on the carpet, sobbing.

Through the tears she fought for a way out, for a way to forget everything. She wanted to forget who she was, forget what had happened to her, and forget the past.

She sat leaning against the bed, knees drawn up to her chest. The room was too perfect. She wished she could rewind the clock and go back to the time when her dad was still alive, when her life had been perfect too.

Her thoughts were interrupted by a light tapping on the bedroom door. Jay straightened up quickly and said, 'Yes?'

Sita peered in from the doorway. 'You are awake.' She stepped inside the room and looked around, shaking her head. 'It is a very young girl's room. Amala loved every shade of pink. I should have redecorated it after Amala left home, but it was always one of those less urgent jobs.' She laughed softly. 'Priyanka, my granddaughter, loves it, of course. She is so like her mother.' She turned her eyes to Jay. 'What are you reading?'

'Nothing. Sorry. I was only looking at the books,' Jay said apologetically. 'I love reading.' She didn't want Sita to think she was snooping, or trying to steal something. The hardback edition of *Little Women* was still in her hands, and she quickly returned it to the bookcase.

'Amala was passionate about books too. Priyanka not so much yet, but she is still young.'

'I had to leave my books behind,' Jay said regretfully. Her books were her most treasured possessions.

'Books are easy to replace,' Sita said matter-of-factly, but Jay noticed the slight catch in her voice.

'Let's go downstairs. I've warmed up some soup.'

Jay followed her down to the kitchen, beginning to feel anxious. Sita would want her to leave soon after the meal, and it would be dark by then. She still had to find somewhere safe to spend the night. Parks were usually deserted, but some of the nicer ones were locked up at night. There was a small park near the library, but she couldn't remember how far it was from Sita's house, and the way her legs kept shaking, she wasn't sure how far they'd take her.

Sita ladled the soup into bowls. The table had been set for two, with warm pitta bread in a basket, a pot of hummus and some green olives. Jay sipped her soup slowly, drawing it out for as long as she could, while Sita chatted about herself. She knew Sita was keeping a close eye on how much she was eating. The soup went down; the pitta bread more slowly.

Once they had finished eating, Jay was convinced Sita would ask her to leave soon.

'Tell me about yourself, Jay. I may have been the matron, but I knew very little about most of the girls really.'

Jay didn't want to talk about herself, she wanted to ask for a packet of painkillers and some money – a ten-pound note to see her through the next couple of days, while she worked out what to do. But it felt wrong asking for money.

She picked up the plates and bowls and took them to the sink. She turned the tap on to wash them up while she plucked up the courage to ask.

'Come and sit down. I will do those later.'

'It's the least I can do. You've been so kind to me.'

'No, please leave them, Jay. I absolutely insist.'

She sat back down, twiddling her fingers, picking at her bruised knuckles, and looking anywhere but at Sita.

'Do you have any brothers or sisters?' Sita asked her. 'I don't recall you having any while you were at St Montague's.'

That one she could answer. 'No. I'm an only child.'

'Are you still at the school?'

Jay shook her head.

'Where do you go now?'

'Kingswell Secondary.'

'Oh, I don't think I know that one. Do you like it there?'

'Not half as much as St Monty's. I've got used to it now. I – I had to leave St Monty's . . .'

'Why was that?' Sita probed gently.

'When my dad died, three years ago, we had to move.' Jay's voice started trembling. 'Everything changed after that,' she whispered.

'Oh, I am so sorry, Jay. I really am. That was after I left. I retired at Christmas that year.'

'You left a term before I did.'

Sita reached out and squeezed Jay's arm. The tears came without warning. Jay thought she had done with crying. She brushed them away with her sleeve, embarrassed.

Sita went out of the room and returned with a box of tissues. 'I am very sorry, Jay. I wondered if it might have been your fa–'

'My dad? He would never have hurt me. Never!' Jay sobbed. 'He would never have let anyone do anything to me! It wouldn't have happened. None of it!'

Sita came round the table and held her tenderly while she cried. It was a relief to cry again, even though it stung her eye. Jay hadn't really known much about Sita when she was at school, other than that she was the matron, but already she wished she was her daughter. She wished she was Amala. She wished she was anyone but Jayalakshmi Sharma.

'It's OK, Jay.' Sita squeezed Jay's shoulder. 'It may not feel like it now, but time will heal you. Your eye will be fine. The bruises will fade away and disappear, and you will be as good as new again.'

As good as new.

Oh, how she wished that could be true. 'You don't understand,' she cried. 'I'll never ever be the same again. No one can love me now. No one would want to – to touch me. I'm – I'm... not me any more. I'll never be as good as new.'

There was a moment's pause as Sita absorbed Jay's words. 'Yes, you will! You are not dead, Jay. You are very much alive, and therefore you can heal.'

It wasn't the response Jay expected. 'How? You can't heal this! No one can heal me. It's too late.' Her voice became smaller and smaller. She wrapped her arms around herself and sank down to the floor. She wanted to be back upstairs in the pink room where it was safe and quiet.

'Listen to me, Jay. I want to help you. You are not alone. Come and sit down at the table. I need you to talk to me.' She helped her up off the floor and into a chair.

'Jay, even if you don't want to tell me what actually happened, and I can understand if you don't, you must tell me something about the circumstances.'

The circumstances? They didn't mean anything. They didn't matter. The only thing that mattered was the thing she could not speak about.

Sita pressed Jay again, and Jay knew she would have to tell her something, anything. So, in halting sentences, Jay told Sita all about how she and her mum ended up living at 42 Primrose Avenue.

CHAPTER 14

'Jay?'

Jay didn't want to speak any more. She'd told Sita about her life since leaving St Monty's, about the lead-up to the party, but that was as far as she could go.

Sita's voice called her back to the present. But it was just another place she did not want to be. The past held nothing, the present even less. What could the future possibly hold?

Sita leaned forward and pressed her hand on Jay's arm. Her fingers were long and thin. There was a plain gold band on her ring finger. 'Tell me what happened last night, Jay.'

'I don't want to talk any more.'

'Jay, someone hurt you terribly. Please talk to me

about what happened.'

Jay shook her head. 'Why do you care anyway?'

'Because you are in so much pain and need help. Because you are here in my home. Do I need a reason to care?' Sita ended in exasperation. 'All right, tell me about your room. They put you in the cellar, you said.'

'You don't believe me, do you?'

Sita sighed. 'I have no reason to disbelieve you, Jay.' She got up to put the kettle on. She'd spent many years working as a matron and only three and a half in retirement, but she'd forgotten how hard it could be to get girls to tell you the real reason why they'd come to your office. 'The more you tell me, the better I can help you, Jay.'

The clock was ticking. It was gone eight o'clock now. It was still light outside, but soon it would fade to darkness. Jay knew she had to either leave now or keep talking. Maybe Sita wouldn't ask her to leave if it got dark. She would let her stay the night, wouldn't she? She'd already let her sleep in her daughter's old room. Then Jay could slip out early in the morning and have the whole day to find somewhere, somewhere to hide until she'd worked out what to do. 'I did think Aunty Vimala was going to stick me in a smelly, dark cellar, but when we got down there I found they'd had it converted – into a gym. My room was at the far end of the gym.'

Sita nodded at her to go on. Drawing the truth out was going to be a long, slow process, but the one thing Sita had was time.

'I thought my uncle and aunt had suddenly become fitness fanatics. But the gym wasn't for them. It was for . . .' Jay's voice trailed off.

'It was for who, Jay?'

Jay's eyes shone with tears. Her bottom lip trembled. 'It was for their eldest son,' she said, and quickly moved on. 'You wanted to know about my room. Well, it was big compared to the one in the flat, but bare – like it was just going to be a storage room and they'd kitted it out for me in a rush, with some second-hand stuff. Mum could have shared with me, but Aunty Vimala insisted she take the attic room.'

Sita set the mugs of tea down on the table. 'That must have been hard for both of you.'

'It wouldn't have been, if she'd come down to see me occasionally. But she never had time. She had her jobs, all the cooking and cleaning for Aunty Vimala, and doing her course.'

'Her course?'

'That was one of the reasons we moved there. Mum was doing part-time training to be a teacher again. A maths teacher. She already had a degree in maths from India.'

'Well, that is very admirable.'

Jay didn't say anything.

'I remember your mum well, Jay. Neela. She organized the summer fair for about three years. A very beautiful woman, and so nice. I remember your dad too, but not as well.'

'You wouldn't recognize her now.'

'Oh, I know a few years have gone by, but I'm sure I would.'

'No. She's changed. Completely. You wouldn't recognize her. She's like a mouse – no, like the shadow of a mouse. She's . . .' Jay fell quiet.

Sita changed the subject. 'What about your friends?'

'I don't see Molly any more. It was too hard, too far . . . But I've got two good friends at Kingswell: Matt and Chloe. I was supposed to meet Matt this morning . . .' Jay's voice trailed away again.

'I could call him for you if you like.'

'No! I can't see him now. You can't call him. Please.'

'OK, I won't. It's all right. It was only a suggestion, Jay. But he was your friend. A close friend, I am guessing?'

A close friend.

Would it have been easier if that was the simple truth?

'For a long time, yes.' Jay swallowed hard, feeling the familiar prick of tears in her eyes. 'Oh God,' she whispered hoarsely. 'I've lost everything. Everything.'

She put her hands over her face to hide her tears and pain from Sita. Her shoulders heaved as she cried.

'If he is as good a friend as you say he is, he will understand. He will want to help you.'

Jay remembered how happy he'd been that she was moving to Primrose Avenue, because it was much closer to his house.

And what had they ever done, apart from hold hands? They'd found a way of hanging out by hiding in dark corners of coffee shops where she knew she wouldn't be recognized by anyone. She'd grabbed a few hours after her Saturday shift at the supermarket to hang out with him at his house, where everything was normal. Where Matt's older sister was allowed to have her boyfriend over, where Matt's parents treated her like one of the family, like a regular teenager – where they were allowed to go up to his room and listen to music. Where no one was suspicious, controlling, demanding. Where you were allowed to be yourself.

Where she'd never come to any harm.

Jay covered her face with her hands and moaned. Now it was too late. Too late for her and Matt. He would not, could not, want her now.

Sita took hold of Jay's hands and gently pulled them away from her face. 'Who was it? Who did this to you, Jay? Tell me his name. Was it Matt?'

'No! Not Matt. It could never be Matt.'

'Well then say who it was. Say his name.'

But Jay couldn't say it. She didn't want to see his face.

'You are far away from him. He cannot find you here. No one will hurt you here. Tell me, does your mother know what's happened?'

'No.' She started shivering. Sita fetched a blanket and wrapped it close around her.

'Have you seen her today?'

Jay shook her head.

'Then we must talk to her,' Sita said firmly.

'No! I – I – can't, Sita. Please . . .'

'Then I will. I will speak to her, if you'll allow me to,' Sita suggested. 'I will only tell her as much as you want me to, but we must talk to her very soon.'

'No. I don't want her to know. Not about any of it. Please don't tell her, Sita. She'll be . . . she'll be so ashamed of me. You know she will. She won't understand. But it wasn't my fault.'

Sita shook her head vehemently. 'No, Jay, no, she will never be ashamed of you. And she will know that it was not your fault. She will want to do everything in her power to help you. You know that, Jay. You know that she will.'

'She won't care.'

'She will care more than anybody.'

'You don't understand. She – she abandoned me.'

Sita took Jay's hands in hers and said softly, 'Jay, she will not want to stay in that house if the man who raped you lives there. She will want to be with you, wherever you are.'

There it was. That terrible word. Sita had guessed it and now she had gone and said it aloud. Jay tried not to hear it, but it was too late. She tried to concentrate on what Sita was saying, but she couldn't hear any more. She teetered on the brink of the void, wanting to fall into its numbness.

'Jay? Jay?'

'Leave me alone. Please, leave me alone,' she whispered, curling in on herself.

'No. I cannot do that, Jay. Let me help you.'

'Please, Sita. I'll go now.' She stumbled out of the kitchen, swaying from side to side, unable to control her movements. It felt as though the world was closing in on her. 'You don't have to worry about me any more. I'm going. I'm sorry to have caused you all this trouble.'

She shrugged off Sita's hand and almost made it to the front door. Sita caught hold of her and pulled her into a hug and held her tight. 'I want to help you. I really do.'

'But I'm hateful,' Jay sobbed.

'No, no.' She stroked Jay's hair. 'You are only a child.'

Sita drew her back to the kitchen.

After a long while of holding her, Sita tried again. 'We must tell your mother. I know it will be hard, but it is necessary.' Even though Jay didn't respond, Sita pressed on. 'It is nine o'clock now. Let me call her, before it gets too late. Does she drive?'

'No. We don't have a car.'

'That's not a problem. I will go and pick her up and bring her here.'

'No,' Jay wailed. 'I can't see her. Please don't do that. Please, Sita. Please.'

'You cannot let her stay there, can you, Jay? What do you think she is doing right now?'

'I don't know. I don't care.'

'You do care. You know she is waiting for you.'

'So?'

'Which is why we have to call her, at the very least.'

'Then she'll want to see me, and I don't want to see her. And then she won't want to go back to that house.'

'Of course she would not want to stay there. I have enough spare rooms for both of you here. I'll get a piece of paper and I want you to write down her telephone number and the address.' She took a notepad and a pencil from the kitchen drawer and placed them in front of Jay.

Jay picked up the pencil. It was painful and awkward writing with her bruised, trembling hands and the result was a barely legible scrawl.

Sita put her reading glasses on. 'Is that number 42?

Jay nodded.

'Primrose Avenue,' Sita read out. 'I've lived in this part of London for a long time, but I don't know a Primrose Avenue. Whereabouts is that?'

'It's in Kingsbury. The house is not far from Mayfield Park.'

Sita raised her eyebrows and peered at Jay over the top of her reading glasses. 'Is that near where you go to school? In Kingsbury?'

'Yes.'

'Do you have any idea how far you walked?'

'It wasn't far enough,' Jay said.

Where would she be now, if she hadn't bumped into her old matron? she wondered. Far enough away that she would never have to face her mum, Jay thought.

'Yes it was. They would never have found you. But it is lucky that I did.'

Sita made the call from the phone in the hallway, while Jay half-listened from the kitchen. She could imagine her mum sitting in her shoebox of a room at the top of No.42, wondering where her daughter had got to, waiting; prepared to wait the whole night if need be. She could imagine her increasingly anxious expression as the minutes and hours ticked by, and the frown and the sudden fear as the strange number came up on her phone. So few people had Neela's mobile number, a handful at most. And then Jay could almost taste her mother's fear as she answered this call, and a stranger told her that something had happened to her child.

'Oh hello, this is Sita Anandhati. Am I speaking to Mrs Neela Sharma? . . . I don't know whether you remember me, but I was the matron up at St Montague's . . . Yes. I'm retired now, but I'm actually calling on behalf of your daughter, Jay. Yes, yes, she's all right. She is here with me. She is safe.'

The two women spoke for some time. Sita was very good. She kept her promise and didn't go into any details on the phone, but it was decided that her mother pack her things and wait for Sita at the end of the road. Her mum must have guessed something really big was up, because she agreed to Sita's plan immediately – even telling her to hurry up.

'No, no, I will not be long at all,' Sita had said patiently. 'I will be driving a white Peugeot. Bring everything you need – there is a lot of space. No, it is no problem, and yes, Mrs Sharma – Neela – I am leaving right this minute.'

Jay felt the tiniest twinge of guilt. Her mother was so desperate to see her that she was ordering a stranger around. It was so unlike her. Did she already know? No, it was impossible. Ash might have mentioned something about what had happened earlier. But he didn't know everything.

Her mum had sent Ash down to check that Jay was OK, but in the morning she would have seen the state of the gym for herself. That might have worried her. But only because of the mess it was in.

What had her mother been thinking all day?

CHAPTER 15

It had started as a routine Sunday morning for Neela. She was still tired from working in the kitchen for most of the day of the party, but she'd had so many willing hands helping out, that in the end the ladies had their own party, in the kitchen. The day had been a success and she was happy for Balji. She had not minded working hard – it was her way of saying thank you to him for taking her and Jay in. He'd refused to take any money from her for rent, but of course Vimala had made sure that she paid her way in cleaning and cooking and shopping.

Neela did not mind. It was a small price to pay for a roof over their heads and a safe, stable environment for her daughter. She only wished Jaya felt the same way.

Neela got ready for the temple and went downstairs, to see if Jaya would go with her. It would be good for her daughter to give her thanks at the temple. God had been kind to them, finally providing them with a safe home – even if her daughter was too spoiled to appreciate it. But that was not entirely Jaya's fault, Neela acknowledged. She blamed herself for it too. She had allowed her daughter too much freedom when she was younger, and little or no guidance in their culture and traditions.

The stench of stale alcohol and cigarettes hit Neela as she descended the stairs to the cellar, but it did not prepare her for the dreadful sight that met her eyes.

She cringed as she picked her way across the once shiny wooden floor, now littered with empty beer bottles and sticky with each step. Deven and his friends had carried on with their own party down here, after all the other guests had left. Had she not been on her way out, she would have started cleaning it up there and then, but she was dressed up and already late for the temple. She couldn't imagine how Jaya had got any sleep with this party going on right next door to her bedroom, and now she regretted not coming down herself to see if she was all right.

There was no answer when she knocked on Jaya's door, so she let her daughter sleep in that morning. Jaya could give her thanks at the temple the following Sunday.

Neela arrived back from the temple around half past one, and Vimala had immediately asked her if she would mind tidying up downstairs.

'I would do it myself, Neela, but you know how my back is, and the boys are out.'

Vimala grimaced dramatically as she rubbed the small of her back, demonstrating how painful it was.

Of course Neela did not mind cleaning up. She would squeeze her college work in later. When she got downstairs Jaya's door was ajar, so she called out to her, but there was no answer. Neela wondered where she had gone. She was not overly concerned, as Jaya always came home on time, and if she was going to be out for long, she would have told her beforehand, or sent a text. That reminded Neela – she hadn't charged her phone. As soon as she finished cleaning up, she would go and plug it in. It was, as usual, on her bedside table.

Cleaning up took much longer than she thought it would. She placed all the beer bottles in a box, shocked at how many there were. She didn't realize that Deven had had so many friends down here. She would have appreciated Jaya's help now. She had always helped her out, ever since her father had died. She was a good girl really, headstrong like her father, but with his good heart too, and cleverer than both her parents.

Neela knew Jaya was very unhappy living in this

house, but she also knew that her daughter was too young to see the whole picture. In the long run, living here for a few years would save them enough money for her to be able to help put Jaya through university. In the meantime, she would qualify as a teacher and be able to save more. Eventually they would be on their feet and beholden to no one. Then they could live where they wanted. But not now.

She had sometimes wondered whether it would not have been better to return to her family in India after her husband died. Now, three years later, she knew she had done the right thing by staying here. Soon, she and her daughter would be free, whereas back home she would have been tied to her family for ever and Jaya would have been an outsider. It would have been different if she and her husband had raised Jaya in a more traditional way.

Neela doubted very much that she would play any part whatsoever in choosing Jaya's husband. Besides, Jaya was turning into a beautiful young woman who was more than capable of making her own future, without the meddling of busybodies like her. The thought of anyone trying to interfere with Jaya's plans raised a smile to her lips.

A glint in the corner of the room, behind the running machine, caught her eye. She crouched down, reaching in with her hand, and brought out a thin gold chain. It was broken – snapped midway, with the clasp still intact – but she recognized it. She reached back in and groped around on the floor under the machine, but could not find the gold-heart locket that used to hang from it. She put the chain in her pocket and carried on cleaning, wondering how it had snapped like that. Jaya loved the necklace and she rarely took it off. The locket must be in her room, Neela decided.

Neela finished cleaning one side of the gym and moved on to the other side. She found the locket lodged between the dumb-bells. She gently rubbed it with a cleaning cloth until it shone again, but she knew something was not right. Jaya would never have lost it in this way. It was too precious to her. She would have got down on her hands and knees and searched until she had found it.

Something was not right.

Neela abandoned the cleaning.

She pushed Jaya's door open and went inside, looking for something – anything, just a sign telling her that everything was all right. The room was tidy – too tidy. Neela's eyes alighted on the bedside table. There was no book there. Even before her daughter had learned to read, she would always keep a book next to her, looking at the pictures until she could read the words. Jaya also had a peculiar habit of reading a few books at the same time. She always had a bedside book, another book for her bag, and, before they came to Primrose Avenue, there was yet another book for the living room.

She shut Jaya's door, feeling anxious now, and went quickly upstairs to check her phone. The battery was completely dead, so she plugged it in to charge, turned it on, and checked for messages. But there was nothing: no messages, no missed calls. It was possible Jaya did not know she had lost her necklace, but deep down Neela did not believe that. They had been forced to sell everything to make ends meet after her husband had died. The necklace was Jaya's tenth birthday present, and it had ended up in the pawn shop, but on Jaya's thirteenth birthday, Neela had bought it back from the shop and given it to Jay. The look on her daughter's face when she opened the box was something she would always treasure. Her sheer joy – over a gift she had received three years earlier – had filled Neela with emotion. Perhaps her daughter was not as spoiled as she thought.

Belatedly, she realized that she had neglected Jaya for too long. She decided to finish her college work before Jaya got home, so she could spend some time with her. She would go down to her room and 'hang out'. She couldn't remember the last time she had done that.

The work was easy – lesson plans, which she usually

enjoyed preparing – but today she was distracted. Her mind constantly flitted back to the broken chain and the locket – and how they had ended up in different parts of the gym. She finished up and stowed the file in her bag, ready for college the next evening, promising herself that she was not going to miss any more lectures. She had missed so many, with the lead-up to the party keeping her busy in the kitchen. Neela had to pass her exams in July, because she wanted to keep her end of the bargain with her daughter and eventually leave Primrose Avenue. She also wanted Jaya to be proud of her.

She checked her phone again. Still no message from Jaya. She sent her a text, asking her to call. By six o'clock, there was still no response. Neela went down to the cellar to check that Jaya hadn't come home and gone straight to her room, but it was empty. She heard noises in the kitchen, and thought maybe Jaya had returned home hungry.

It wasn't Jaya but Ashok, spilling the contents of the fridge out on to the kitchen counter in a messy attempt at making a sandwich.

'Here, let me help you,' she offered. 'Would you like me to cook something proper for you, Ashok? I don't think your mother and father have eaten yet, so I can make something for you all.'

'It's OK, Aunty. Um, actually, I think they've

gone out to some friends, or something,' Ash said apologetically.

'Oh, I see. But I can still make something for you.'

'I can manage. Thanks anyway, Aunty.'

'Have you seen Jaya today, Ashok?'

'No, sorry, I haven't. I knocked on her door this morning to do that bolt for her, but I think she was out, or still asleep.'

'A bolt?' Neela repeated, puzzled. 'She wanted a bolt put on her door?'

'Um, yeah. You know, with the party and everything, and all Deven's friends down there.'

An alarm bell began to ring in Neela's head. Deven was a handful, but . . . 'Did you check on her last night, Ashok? Was she in her room, or in the gym room? She wasn't with them, was she?'

'Yeah, I saw her. She was OK.'

Neela noticed he was avoiding her eyes, so she pressed him. 'Were they bothering her, Ashok?'

'Well, you know, they'd had a fair bit to drink.'

'What did they do?'

'Um, they were hassling her.'

Neela's hand flew to her mouth. 'What? How? What were they doing, Ashok?'

'Just messing about. It's OK, she was all right. I got them to leave. They went to a party somewhere else and Jay went to bed. I don't know what time Deven got back in, but he was in a real state this morning – and it wasn't just the drink.'

'What do you mean?'

'I think he got into a fight or something. Typical,' Ash said, with unfeigned disgust. 'He was covered in scratches and in a filthy mood. Mum was not happy.'

'Oh, I am sorry to hear that. Where is he now?'

'Think he was going to head straight back to uni. Good riddance!'

'Ashok, you should not speak that way about him,' she admonished, although, in truth, she did not care for Deven very much herself. 'No matter what he does, he is still your brother.'

'Sorry, Auntyji, but, you know, he *is* a real idiot.' She watched him load the fridge back up, and then he left with a mumbled: 'Got homework to finish, but if Jay still wants the bolt on, I'll do it for her tomorrow.'

'Thank you, Ashok.'

It was after seven o'clock now, and there was still no word from Jaya. Neela's messages remained unanswered. This was not like her daughter. There was something wrong. Neela had felt it all day – since she had seen the broken heart necklace. The conversation with Ashok troubled her too. She had not even considered the possibility that Deven and his friends would be unkind to Jaya. She knew Jaya did not care for Deven, but Deven had always treated her like a younger sister, in the past.

Yet Jaya's attitude continued to baffle Neela – she could not understand why she so desperately wanted to leave this lovely house. Jaya always said that living in the flat was far better than living here, which Neela could not understand at all. The flat had been shabby, the area not so nice. What had been so good about living there? She wondered whether it reminded Jaya too much of their old lives. They had once lived in a beautiful house, with a pool, a large garden, and so much more.

Or perhaps it was a teenage thing, a phase Jaya was going through? Neela sighed. She had tried her best for Jaya. She did not know the cause of her daughter's unhappiness. Perhaps she would never know.

She went back to Jaya's room and switched on the light, acknowledging that it wasn't the homeliest room. Only the beautiful bedcovers from their old home lifted the surrounding bleakness. When she thought about how much they had cost, it horrified her now. Jaya's collection of pens and pencils lay scattered under the desk and the ruler was broken. Neela gathered them up and put them back on the desk, placing a book in front of them so they wouldn't roll off the table again. She tossed the broken ruler in the bin, reminding herself to bring her own one down for Jaya to use. Then she stopped. There was something in the bin that looked like – no, it could not be . . . She looked again. They looked like long tresses of hair, lying coiled at the bottom.

She bent down for a closer look. There was no mistake – it was her daughter's hair.

'Jaya!' she gasped, stumbling back in shock. She sat down on the bed, and saw the cracked mirror. Her hand flew to her mouth to stifle a sob.

Was her daughter this unhappy, this angry? Had she decided to punish her, by destroying the things she loved? Why else would she cut off her beautiful hair and leave it in the dustbin for her mother to find?

Had she run away?

She looked for Jaya's bag. It was not there. Neela didn't know what to do next. Should she call the police and tell them her daughter was missing? They would ask her how long she had been missing, and then what would she say?

She did not know how long Jaya had been gone for. Ashok was the last person to see her, last night. Neela had not seen her since . . . since Saturday afternoon. Anyway, what would the police do? Nothing, in all probability. They would tell her she was being silly and jumping to conclusions. They would also ask if there were any problems at home, if they had argued . . .

In the end, they would simply reassure Neela and tell her that Jaya would probably be home soon, that it was still early. They would remind her that teenagers lost track of time when they were with their friends, and despite her protestations that her daughter wasn't like that, they would not take her seriously. Not yet. Perhaps not even until tomorrow.

If Jaya had really run away, where would she go? She had no one to run to, and no money. Neela clasped her hands together in front of her, and began a silent prayer for her daughter.

Every few minutes, she thought she heard someone upstairs and raced up to check. She checked the attic and the garden too, just in case. She did not know what else to do.

By eight o'clock – with no word, no text, no contrite telephone call, no telephone call at all – she began to get angry at Jaya, for putting her through this unnecessary worry. All the girl had to do was call her and tell her she was all right. It didn't take more than a minute to do that, no matter how much fun she was having.

And then Neela reminded herself that Jaya had never done this before. There had to be a good reason.

Jaya did have one very good friend, that English boy called Matt. Maybe she was with him. They were very close. Was it possible they were more than just friends? Jaya was not that young any more – she was fifteen years old. Neela wished she knew where the boy lived; she wished she had asked Jaya for his phone number.

She felt stupid, because despite the many hours he had spent in their flat, she did not even know his surname.

Neela paced around the room. She knew she had to talk to Jaya, explain everything properly, and make her understand why they had to live here. Above all, she had to impress upon her that it was a temporary arrangement. And Neela finally realized that she had to find time to be with her daughter. Jaya was right – their lives had drifted so far apart. She would buy a cheap second-hand television and put it here in Jaya's room, and then they could spend their evenings together, as they used to in the flat.

She would also suggest painting the room, as Jaya did when they had moved to the flat. It had not even occurred to her here. It would have made the room feel nicer for Jaya. Tomorrow, she would suggest it, and also check with Vimala that it was OK to paint the room. There would be objections, but Neela would not let them get in the way. But the room needed more than a simple coat of paint to make it feel homely.

She smoothed the bedcovers down and noticed some dark speckles and a few smears on the pillow. Chocolate, she thought, knowing Jaya's sweet tooth. She would put fresh sheets on the bed while she was waiting. It would be good to do something, rather than stand idle and worry. Besides, she knew Jaya never got around to these things. Her daughter had never minded running round the flat with the vacuum cleaner and the duster, and even washing up, but loading and unloading the washing machine, never. Neela did those things, until they had moved here – and she had not done it once for Jaya since then.

She took clean sheets from the top of the wardrobe and placed them on the chair, ready, and then removed the pillowcases. She dropped them on the floor and began to pull the poppers apart on the duvet cover, wondering whether it was too late to put the washing machine on. With the duvet displaced, she caught a glimpse of the sheets beneath. She gasped in shock, dropping the duvet.

Then her phone rang.

CHAPTER 16

Jay was back in the kitchen, waiting for the front door to open. Only the ticking clock broke the silence. Every time she thought she heard the door, a surge of panic rushed through her, threatening to engulf her.

She would get up from the table then and pace round the kitchen, running her hands through her shorn locks, pulling and tugging at the ends.

She was trying hard not to imagine the conversation taking place in Sita's car, trying not to picture the look on her mum's face as Sita explained everything. Jay shuddered violently and choked back a sob. She couldn't bear to think about it.

She opened the back door and stepped into the garden. The security lamp came on in a blaze of light. She followed the meandering path up the garden and through the trees. The garden was neat and tidy, like the house.

There was a shed at the back. It was large, almost the size of a log cabin. It had two glass windows on either side of the door, with a bigger window running along the side, and a covered veranda at the front with a little deck and a small table and two chairs. A bird feeder hung off the post at one end of the veranda, and a hanging basket, resplendent with flowers, was suspended from the other. There was a clear view of most of the garden, but the house was slightly obscured by a weeping willow.

Jay tried the shed door – it was unlocked. She went inside and groped around for the light switch. She found it and flicked it on. The shed was full of the usual stuff: gardening tools, a parasol propped up in one corner, more garden furniture, bags of compost and seed trays, and a lawnmower. On the shelves were tins of paint, empty plant pots stacked one inside the other, a ladder suspended horizontally along the wall, and a neatly coiled orange cable that looked as though it belonged to the lawnmower. Everything was neat and orderly, but she found it unsettling. The mundane trappings of an ordinary life, a life that had been snatched away from her – they made her feel like an interloper who had no right to be there.

She hit the light switch and went back outside. She

sat down on the rickety garden chair, wondering if she should leave before they got back. But it was dark now. Where would she go? She could curl up in someone's front garden, behind the wheelie bins or bushes, and leave at first light in the morning. She would have to sleep rough for a while, maybe for a long while. She'd have to pass herself off as an eighteen year old and get a job doing something, anything; live the life of someone who had nothing.

The security light went off, and, in the sudden darkness, the awful memory of what had been done to her came shrieking back into her head, unbidden and unwanted, and terrible thoughts crowded her mind, clamouring to be heard. She could not shut them out.

They were angry thoughts, thoughts full of rage, revulsion; a deep, scorching hatred burned through her; thoughts of *him* and how she despised him, loathed him, detested him.

But her rage demanded more: it wanted her to hurt him badly, maim him, scar him for ever, but even the idea of that wasn't enough.

She wanted him dead.

She wanted to kill him with her bare hands; she wanted to tear that smirk apart with her nails, shred his face into ragged pieces of flesh. She wanted to destroy him – the way he had destroyed her. The girl with the brilliant future was gone. She was never coming back.

The girl left in her place didn't have a future, could see nothing but his leering face laughing at her.

Jay wanted revenge.

Her fury was interrupted by voices from the kitchen. She jumped up, knocking the chair over, and stumbled off. She didn't want to hear their voices. She needed to hold on to the rage and the anger; it empowered her. It was the only thing that made her feel anything. She ran to the back fence, searching for a back gate, a way out . . . but she'd left it too late.

She heard Sita calling her. There was nothing else for it but to go back in the house. The women's voices chased away the fading remnants of her rage, and left her empty, purposeless and vulnerable again.

Her mother was standing on the other side of the kitchen table. Jay watched her mum's hands as they flew to her mouth in horror. 'Jaya! My God!'

Jay shrank back. She knew she should have run away before her mum saw her. She didn't need this. She already knew she had a split, fat lip and that her right eye had practically closed over. Her scarecrow haircut told the rest of the story.

But her mum of all people should have been able to pretend that she was still her beautiful little girl and not some misshapen creature that had escaped from a freak show.

'Jaya,' her mum said again, her voice breaking. This time her mother was unable to hold back the tears. She came towards Jay, eyes streaming, hands outstretched, but Jay pulled a chair out from under the table and sat down quickly, before her mother could hug her.

She wanted to scream, *Don't touch me.*

'Mum,' she said tightly, refusing to look at her.

Jay's manoeuvre stopped her mother in her tracks and a tense silence descended until Sita broke it with, 'Please sit down, Neela.' Sita filled the silence with the clatter of cups and saucers.

'*Beti*, my darling,' her mother began, reaching across the table for her hands.

Jay took her hands off the tabletop and clasped them in her lap defensively. She couldn't let her mum touch her. She didn't want to be touched by her. The kitchen suddenly felt too hot. Her hands had gone all clammy and her breathing had quickened. She had to get out.

'I have to go to the bathroom,' she mumbled, and fled – ignoring the look that passed between the two women.

In the bathroom, she took her time. The cold water was soothing. She let the tap run for ages, splashing her face, her hands, and her arms. She leaned over the sink and let the tears mingle with the water as it rushed down the plughole in a swirl.

When she finally forced herself to go back to the kitchen to face the two women, it was Sita who did the talking. Her mum simply looked at her, tight-lipped and pale, tears running down her face. They seemed to have decided lots of things.

'Jay, you must understand that we would not be acting responsibly if we did not do the right things for you,' Sita started.

'What do you mean by the "right things"?'

'Well, there is a procedure we must follow. Apart from calling the police, we must call a doctor, obviously, and . . .'

Jay interrupted her. 'For the morning-after pill? In case I'm pregnant? He didn't use a condom, so I could have an STD too, maybe even AIDS!'

It may well have been true, but she'd spat the words out in pure spite – and they had the desired effect: her mum was so shocked she could barely bring herself to look at Jay.

As all the other 'right things' were outlined to her, Jay wished she could simply disappear. She wished she had left before they had returned. It was too late to run away now. She began to shrink, and by the time Sita picked up the phone, Jay could no longer find her voice. She turned in on herself, feeling small and tiny and completely defenceless.

The calls were made quickly. 'Yes, she has only

recently turned fifteen,' Jay heard Sita say. She blocked her ears to the rest of the words.

All the things she was afraid of – doctors, police, shrinks, the works – would soon be pitching up on the doorstep.

The doorbell began to ring and, one after the other, they traipsed into the house, leaving her to take refuge in the only place that was left – the empty, blank void inside her, where she felt nothing and nothing could touch her.

It was two o'clock in the morning and Jay was lying in bed. Her mother had been in to check on her a few times, but Jay pretended to be asleep. Sita had given her mum the room next door, and they had all gone to bed, but it was clear that no one would be getting any sleep that night. Too much had happened. The house had been full of people milling about, talking quietly and walking on tiptoes. In the kitchen, endless cups of tea were made and gratefully received, and plates of biscuits disappeared as fast her mum could fill them. Neela was on tea duty, because Jay wouldn't let her stay with her. Instead, Sita stayed beside Jay the whole time.

Two police officers arrived first, to take a preliminary statement. They had the gall to be disappointed that she'd washed and cleaned herself so thoroughly, and they couldn't conceal their irritation when she refused to talk to them after that. Sita had to remind them that Jay was only just fifteen. They apologized, and told them that two women police officers were arriving soon. They said they had an early evidence kit with them, and all Jay needed to give them in the meantime was a mouth swab and a urine sample. She gave them the urine sample, and then locked herself in the bathroom.

The two female officers were no less easy to face. There were interminable questions. They had pulled it all out of her, not allowing her the refuge of a monosyllabic response. It went on and on until every sordid detail of that entire night was logged and filed – all that she could remember; much more than she wanted to remember.

Later, she caught sight of the bin liner. She saw her mother present it to them, like a gift, with the edge of her no longer pristine white-lace duvet cover poking shamefully out of the top. Her mother had very thoughtfully brought it along with her. The stained sheet, the smeared pillow, the ripped pyjamas – they were all in there.

Jay ran away to the bathroom and vomited violently.

When she returned to the room, they told her it was 'imperative' that they take her for a medical exam. It was what Jay had feared, what she couldn't face.

'There's a SARC a twenty-minute drive from here. It won't take long, Jay,' the fair-haired policewoman said.

'A SARC?' Sita asked.

'Yes, it's a Sexual Assault Referral Centre. This one is open twenty-four hours. We've called ahead and they have a female doctor waiting,' the officer explained. 'Jay, the man who did this to you needs to be locked away. The evidence is important. It won't take long, I promise.'

Jay endured all the indignities that were required in order for justice to be done. There were endless examinations, the poking and the prodding of the rape kit, the sampling of semen, the extraction of blood.

Apparently it was a cut and dried case. There would be no counter-case, no argument with this kind of evidence. It spoke for itself. The photographs were simply the illustrations that were needed to prove Jay's case. You can't tell a story without pictures. So the shutters of the camera went *click-click* at regular intervals and the flash blinked angrily, snapping pieces of her on to film, permanent images that would be saved, printed and then handed out in sterile courtrooms where they would be fingered until their corners went dog-eared and shabby. Until everyone had seen enough of the image of the broken girl.

Tomorrow, it would be no better. The doctor had

promised to visit her, and she would bring a counsellor with her, and the policewoman said she would be passing by too. There would be more questions, all spoken in that terribly understanding, slightly pitying tone.

When would it stop? Would it ever stop? Would it ever go away? Would they ever leave her alone?

Much later, after they all left, Jay lay in bed, unable to sleep. She thought if she sat up in bed and tried to remember everything they had said and the conversations she'd overheard between them, that it would clear her mind and she would then find sleep. But it didn't work; it was jumbled up and disjointed.

She lay back down and pulled the covers close, shivering even though it was a warm night. During the night, sleep came and went, punctuated by all the things that had been said. It was exhausting, but she could not block the words out.

Because you are a minor, your identity will be protected.

Have no fear, we will be prosecuting him.

The evidence is overwhelming.

He'll go down for this.

We'll pick him up now.

You won't have to see him, love.

Send a squad car over to the house.

It's No.42, Primrose Avenue.

Eventually, she must have fallen asleep, because she woke up to a pink dawn in a pink room, which, before this weekend, would have felt like a lovely dream, except pink did not feel right now. Pink was too nice, too sugary, too pretty for Jay now. Pink was for little innocents, and she wasn't an innocent any more.

She went to the bathroom. Peeing was painful, and her stomach hurt. Her right eye had completely closed over. The cut on her lip was a painful weeping sore. She crept back into bed and curled up, silently moaning, crying without tears.

There would be more faces today – lots of faces, kind voices, sympathetic noises, nodding heads. None of which would help her; none of which soothed her anger or took away her hate.

She wouldn't get out of bed today.

But staying in bed didn't stop them coming. They trooped up to the pink room, one by one. Jay drew the covers up to her chin. Sometimes she turned her face away from them. By evening, all was quiet again.

She decided to go down for dinner because the alternative was unbearable. Her mother would sit quietly next to her with a tray of food on her lap. She would wait for Jay to wake up so she could help her, feed her, wash her, dress her – anything. But Jay kept her face turned firmly towards the wall.

Her mum had come back later, the clink of crockery alerting Jay to the fact that her mother intended to sit patiently by her bedside again.

But Jay could not bear that closeness. She could not face her mum. She didn't want to see her, speak to her or be with her.

So she went down to the kitchen, swallowed a few mouthfuls of dhal, and told them she was going back to bed, to sleep, and to please leave her alone. They tried to talk to her, engage her, but now that everyone knew everything, there wasn't much to talk about. It had all been said.

The next day, the policewoman came to tell her the good news. Deven had been arrested and charged. He was in custody.

She had smiled and patted Jay's hand as though it was the best news ever, as though it would somehow make her happy. It wasn't going to make everything all better again, she said, but justice was being done. He was getting what he deserved. He would be tried and convicted, placed on the sex-offenders list, and for ever labelled a paedophile, a vicious rapist. He would serve his time.

But Jay didn't greet this news with any sense of relief or satisfaction. Instead, she felt so angry she wanted to scream and rage.

She knew he would be out in a few years, free to roam the world as he pleased. But he would be no different. He would still be the same person, and two or three years in prison would not change that. How could it?

She had wanted to mete out her own justice. She had wanted to exact her revenge in a very different way. It was all she had thought about the past few days – how she would do it, how she would find him, how she would hurt him. It had kept her going through the darkest hours, through the pain and the shame.

Now she had nothing to do, nothing to think about, and nothing to look forward to.

CHAPTER 17

Days drifted from one to the next, without Jay. She lost sense of time. One morning, she was lying in bed when the doorbell rang for the third or fourth time. An insistent visitor. Jay hoped it wasn't anyone to visit her.

She could hear Sita ushering people in, and then her mother's voice greeting them as though they were her best friends. Jay got out of bed, crept to the door and opened it a crack. Her heart sank as her suspicions were confirmed. Mrs Fitzgerald's booming voice was unmistakable. And she had Miss Basma with her.

Jay shut the door quietly and jumped back into bed. She faced the wall and pulled the duvet over her head, hoping that the teachers would have some tea, get the low-down on what had happened, which was obviously why they had come, and then leave when they realized she was sleeping. She couldn't face them.

Mrs Fitzgerald was the deputy head at Kingswell Secondary School. Miss Basma was the school counsellor. She liked her; Jay had spent a lot of time with Miss Basma when she'd started at the school. She had a soft voice, a gentle manner and endless patience. She had eventually coaxed Jay out of the shell she had embedded herself in.

Perhaps she thought she could do it again.

Half an hour passed. Jay hadn't heard the front door again, which meant they were still around.

Faint voices came from the hallway. Were they leaving? She hoped so. She didn't want to see either of them. These teachers knew her too well. They had such high hopes for her: university, maybe even Oxbridge, and a glittering future. She had worked so hard for it.

But no, their footsteps were on the stairs now. They were coming up.

There was a knock on the door. Jay buried her head under the pillow, ignoring it. The knocking continued, louder this time.

They were bound to go away eventually, when she didn't respond. She was sure they wouldn't want to barge in while she was sleeping.

But then the door opened.

'Jaya?' It was her mum.

Jay wanted to strangle her. 'Go away,' she hissed under her breath. Her teachers would never have forced her to see them – but her mother would.

'Oh, if she's asleep, we'll come back another time,' Miss Basma whispered. 'Please don't wake her on our account.'

'No, no, she's not asleep. She's just resting,' Jay heard her mum reply. 'I know she will want to see you.'

Her mother knew nothing. Jay seethed with anger. How could she drag these people into her room without checking with her first? Without even asking her if she was up for visitors?

And there was that tone, that special tone her mother reserved for people like teachers and doctors and the police. Cooperative, respectful, helpful and ever so polite. She was not going to allow Jay to get away with not talking to them. 'Jaya, *beti*, you have some visitors. They have come to see you. I've brought you up some tea.'

Red hot anger seared through Jay. Her mum had to be some kind of idiot to ignore the obvious. Jay did not want to see them. She wanted to take that tea and fling it at her mother. Instead, all she could say was, 'Go away! Leave me alone.'

'Jaya, please talk to them for little while. They have been so worried about you. Here is your tea, Jaya.'

She heard her mum set the cup down on the bedside

table, felt the light touch of her hand on the duvet.

'Come in, please,' her mum said to the teachers.

Jay couldn't ignore them now. She braced herself for their reaction and they reacted very much in the way she expected. Shocked. She *was* a shocking sight. Her face was still a mess of bruises and cuts, and her beautiful long hair had become a mass of short spikes.

Neela took the chair from the desk and placed it next to the bed for Mrs Fitzgerald. She offered to get a chair for Miss Basma, but the school counsellor said she would be fine sitting on the bed. An awkward silence followed.

Jay knew her mum was hovering in the doorway, trying to catch her eye, but Jay refused to look in her direction. She plucked at the duvet, rearranged her pillow, but did not lift her eyes. In the end her mum said, 'I will leave you to talk then,' and closed the door behind her.

'Jay, your mother has told us everything. We wanted to say how terribly, terribly sorry we are,' Mrs F began, her voice all soft and understanding.

It was scary when Mrs F softened her booming voice. Pupils would scatter like bowling pins when they heard her in the corridor, even the usual suspects and assorted loiterers would suddenly decide to stride purposefully into their classes before she got anywhere near them. Her detentions were legendary. Or at least, so Jay had heard. It was common knowledge in her year that Mrs F had a soft spot for Jay.

Mrs Fitzgerald leaned forward. 'Jay, if there is anything – anything at all – we can do to help, you only have to ask. The school will support you in every way it can, of course. The matter will be kept entirely confidential and will go no further than this room. Your teachers have been told that you have had an accident and will be absent from school for a period of time.'

Jay could feel herself choking up. 'Thank you.' Her voice was small and hoarse. She looked down at her hands. The red crescents in her palms stood out boldly like a cluster of moons in a black night. She clenched her fists. She had no intention of going back to Kingswell. Her teachers meant well and they might try to keep it to themselves, but they didn't know how things worked in schools. The kids would find out, somehow.

And they'd never let her forget it.

'We are still some months away from your exams, but you will be given every assistance in preparing for them. You will be able to take your controlled assessments at a later date. You are an exceptionally bright student and we must not let this affect the promising future you rightly deserve.'

'And if need be, Jay, you can delay taking your exams. The exams this year need not impact on your

GCSEs next year,' Miss Basma said gently. Miss Basma had removed her head scarf. Jay had never seen her hair before, as the scarf was never removed at school. Jay supposed it was just in case a male teacher walked in. Miss Basma's hair fell in soft curls to her shoulders, making her look younger.

'Yes, of course. Your final GCSE exams are next year and you're heading for A-stars across the board. That won't change if you delay taking the summer exams this year. You mustn't worry about anything. Just concentrate on getting better.'

What the two women didn't realize was that all the nice, encouraging things they said were about a very different girl. They were talking about the girl with brilliant prospects, but she had disappeared for ever.

As for 'getting better'? What Mrs F didn't understand was that Jay wasn't sick. She didn't have a disease or a long-term illness. The word for what she had couldn't be spoken aloud. And it was something she might not ever be able to recover from.

'Your mother said that you have been assigned a counsellor.' It was Miss Basma's turn again. The lump in Jay's throat was getting bigger and bigger. 'You may not believe it is possible now, but, in time – and with help and support – you will get over this, Jay. Talking about it will help. We talked before. Do you remember?'

How could Jay forget? Jay started at Kingswell at

the beginning of the summer term – there had been no money to finish Year Seven at St Monty's after her dad had died and they had been plunged into poverty – and Miss Basma had asked to see her straightaway, after being made aware of Jay's 'circumstances'. What followed was a whole year of twice-weekly visits to Miss Basma's cramped little office. Months of crying, of refusing to speak to this woman who'd sat patiently, holding her hand, giving her tissues, asking her questions and finally succeeding in drawing her out.

But this was different. This was a different kind of death. How could Jay think of living a normal life again, when everything on the inside was dying? Even Miss Basma wouldn't be able to fix someone who was dead on the inside.

'And I want you to know that I'm here if you need someone to talk to. I'm going to leave you my mobile number.' Miss Basma leaned forward and pressed a card into her hands. 'I want you to call me whenever you need to. Any time. Day or night. Will you do that?' She looked searchingly into Jay's eyes, but Jay had to look away. 'Where's your mobile?' she asked.

'Pardon?'

'Your mobile phone?'

'I don't know. In my bag. Over there.'

Miss Basma passed her the bag. 'Put my number in your phone now, while we're here, so you don't forget.

And remember – you can call me any time, day or night.'

'The battery's almost dead.'

'Do it quickly then.'

Miss Basma was insistent, so Jay did as she was told, although she couldn't see the point of it. The one-way conversation dried up soon after that and the two women left. She sank back into the pillows gratefully. Next time she would make a better job of feigning sleep.

After dinner that evening, Neela paid her another visit. There was a tense silence before her mum spoke.

'Jaya, *beti*, I may have to go back to work tomorrow. They will not allow me any more time off.'

'Fine.' *Great*. Jay hoped she would leave her alone now.

'But I will resign – if you want me to. Sita has said we can stay here for a while, and I can easily find work later. I would rather be with –'

'No. Not on my account. The sooner you go back to work the better.'

'Jaya,' Neela said softly.

Her mum wanted a heart-to-heart.

'I have to sleep.' Inside her head, Jay was screaming at her to go away.

Still her mum didn't leave. 'Jaya, please, do not

keep turning away from me. Listen to me, please. I am so sorry for what happened. So sorry. Please, talk to me. Let me help you. You're my only child. The most precious –'

'Shut up and go away!' Jay cried angrily.

'Jaya, please let me help. I want to help you. You are my baby. I have nothing else.'

'Then you have nothing!' Jay shouted. 'And I don't need your help now! I needed it then.'

'I know, I know. But I thought you were safe, asleep in your room. It had been a long day, so busy for both of us. I thought you went to sleep early. I did not think that –'

Jay glared at her, with eyes full of bitterness and reproach. 'Then you should have listened to me!' she shouted. 'I didn't want to live there! You did. I hated it – I told you that a thousand times. I wanted to leave, and I told you that, too. But, no, you wanted to stay. You didn't listen to me.'

'I know, Jaya, I know, and I explained why we had to live there for a little while. We had no other choice.'

'We could have stayed where we were!'

'You know we could not do that.'

'We could have found somewhere else.'

'But we could not afford it.'

'We could have found something. You didn't even bother looking. You went begging to them instead.'

'Jaya, I did not beg. Your uncle very kindly offered us rooms. I thought it would make your life better.'

'So *this* is better? What happened in that horrible house is better? Live there for free – and the rest doesn't matter? I don't matter?'

'I did not mean that. I never thought anything like this would happen. Please, Jaya.'

'You're my mother – you're supposed to protect me. I kept telling you and telling you, but you didn't listen to me. It's all your fault . . .'

And those words released a rage that she could not control. Words poured out of Jay. Terrible words, damning words. She spat them out; she rolled them into balls of fury and hurled them in her mother's face.

Neela no longer tried to speak, or explain, or reason with her daughter. She accepted the abuse and the blame in silence. Tears ran down her face and she wiped them away, but they kept falling.

And when Jay ran out of words – ran out of breath, her rage spent – all her mum said was: 'I know, Jaya. I am listening now. I am listening.'

'Don't you understand? Haven't you heard a word I said? It's too late. It's too late!'

Neela couldn't contain her emotions any longer, and broke down, sobbing. 'No, no, don't say that, my *beti*, don't say that. I am listening. I am here. I will take care of you now. No one will hurt you ever again.' She tried to put her arms round Jay, wanting to hold her close.

But her mother couldn't take the pain and anger away; they ran too deep through Jay. 'Don't touch me,' Jay hissed through clenched teeth. 'Don't ever touch me.' She was trembling uncontrollably. The only place for her to go where she would be left alone, was deep under the covers.

But nothing could block out her mother's sobs, and the whispered 'I love you, Jaya', before she left the room.

CHAPTER 18

The bedroom door clicked shut. Jay threw the covers off her face. 'But I don't love you any more, Mum,' she whispered.

Being in the house would become much easier now that her mum wasn't going to be around all day, watching her – she wouldn't have to hide from her any more.

Her mum had said that Sita had agreed to let them stay for a while. Jay wondered how long that meant. A few more days? A few weeks?

Then where would they go?

And would she have to go with her mum?

She knew the answer to that question. Of course she'd have to go with her – even if she couldn't stand the sight of her mum, couldn't bear her touch or the sound of her voice.

Jay blamed her as much as *him.*

If her mum had listened to Jay instead of to Aunty Vimala, they would have been sharing a room, and it wouldn't have happened. If Neela had listened when she'd told her that she couldn't bear living there any more because it was turning them into strangers, *it* wouldn't have happened. If her mum had listened to her before that, and found them somewhere else to live, *it* wouldn't have happened. If . . .

Jay could have gone on all afternoon listing all the ifs. But it was too late for ifs; too late to roll back time.

Days passed in a blur of nothingness and half-sleep. She stared at the rose-patterned walls, avoiding eye contact, avoiding any kind of contact.

Nights passed in a haze of nightmares, hot sweats, silent sobbing and tears.

The nightmares were the worst. Jay kept the light on in the hope it would stall them, but it didn't. As soon as she relaxed and shut her eyes – and sometimes that took half the night to achieve – the nightmares would start. Sometimes she would wake up, screaming, fighting the air as though it was pressing down heavily on her. If her mum or Sita heard her screams, one or both of them would come running.

It was always one word, the same word, that she screamed over and over again. *Help*.

Jay never screamed for her mum.

Sita would give her a sip of water and stay a while, and that was OK. Her mum would try to hug her. One night Jay pushed her away so hard, Neela fell back against the desk. She didn't try to hug her again.

It became easier not to sleep at night. Jay read all of Amala's collection of books, losing herself in the innocent little melodramas of the girls at Malory Towers.

She only switched the light off and tried to sleep when dawn broke. But sleep only came in half-hour doses, and it wasn't enough to sustain her.

One day about a week later, Jay went down for a sandwich at lunchtime, to save Sita bringing it up to her. Her mum was at work, and it was a relief knowing she wouldn't be down there, trying to be helpful, giving Jay imploring looks, wanting to talk and to hold her.

The back door was ajar, the sun shining outside. Someone was mowing their lawn.

'Come and sit outside for a while,' Sita said.

Jay shook her head.

'Please yourself. I'll be pottering around out there if you change your mind.'

Jay threw the uneaten half of her sandwich in the bin and washed up their two plates, before sitting back down. Gradually her head sank into her arms on the kitchen table. A fly buzzed annoyingly around her head, but she didn't have the energy to swat it away. Before she knew it, she'd fallen fast asleep.

When she woke it was almost six o'clock. It was still light outside, but the back door was shut. She could hear the television in the living room. It was the first time she had slept almost five hours running since . . . since she'd first walked into Sita's house. And the first time she had not had a nightmare.

Her mum would be back from work soon. Jay eased out of the chair, rubbing the crick in her neck, tiptoed past the living room and back upstairs to the pink room. She wouldn't need to sleep tonight.

'Why don't you put on some clothes and go for a walk? It is a lovely day outside,' Sita suggested. 'There is a park close by. I'll come with you and we can have a nice walk in the sunshine. I have lived here a long time, but that is one thing I have always missed about living in Kenya – the sun and the heat. I have to make the most of the sunshine here.'

It was midday on Friday, and Jay was still walking round the house in pyjamas. She had no appetite, but she forced herself to eat a slice of toast because otherwise Sita would sit there until she'd seen her eat something.

'Or why don't you invite a friend over? I'm going out later on this afternoon, so I won't be in your way.'

'They'll be in school.'

'Oh. You could invite them over after school then.'

Sita never gave up, Jay thought. She was always trying to get her to do something. It would have been a great idea to invite a friend over – except there was no one who Jay wanted to see. Not even Chloe or Matt. Chloe she didn't want to see because she was too perfect. It sounded horrible, but it was true. Chloe had the kind of life that Jay wanted; the kind of life Jay had before her dad died. Normal parents, normal family life, normal everything.

And Matt? Well, she definitely couldn't let him see her. Just thinking about him made her heart ache. She longed for him, for his arms around her and his breath tickling her ear; his voice telling her that everything was going to be all right. But she couldn't call him. She couldn't tell him, she just couldn't. She was scared he wouldn't want to touch her, and even more scared that she might not be able to bear his touch.

'We went over to that house yesterday. Did Neela tell you about it?' Sita said, intruding into her thoughts.

'No.' *That house* could only mean No.42. Why had they gone there? Her heart started beating faster.

'She most probably did not want to upset you, Jay.'

'So, why did you go?'

'For your things from your room, and all your books too – your mother insisted on it. They're on the dining table for now.' There was obviously more to the story, but Sita made her wait while she put her pearl earrings in before continuing. 'It was a most unpleasant experience, even with two police officers with us, but it had to be done. Your mother was hoping your uncle would be there, but unfortunately it was your aunt who answered the door. She made things very difficult.'

'Difficult? How?' Jay had a pretty good idea.

'I'm sure you can guess, Jay. She was abusive, hysterical, refusing to let us in. And then she really went for your mother.' To Jay's astonishment Sita actually threw back her head and laughed.

'What happened then?'

'Your very sweet, mild mother had to be forcibly restrained. Although no one, apart from your aunt of course, was sorry about the couple of very satisfying slaps that did reach their target. The younger brother arrived while we were there. Ashok. He did his best to restrain his mother, but she was out of control. He managed to drag her into the living room so we could go downstairs to get your books. I think he got a few thumps from his mum for his trouble. We packed your things very quickly and the police officers helped us take it all outside. But just as we were about to leave, she came running outside again, the insane woman, and before anyone could stop her, she attacked your mother. But she picked the wrong woman to mess about with, and everything your mum did was done in self-defence.'

It didn't sound like Neela at all. She'd never once stood up to Auntyji, in all the months they'd lived there. 'I – I don't believe you.'

'Oh, yes, it is all true,' Sita insisted, nodding her head. 'You would have been very proud of her, Jay, the way she stood up to that woman.'

It would have been something worth seeing – a sight to treasure. Before the party, Jay would have been over the moon to hear that her mum was finally fighting back. But now . . . she didn't care.

Still, it was something, Jay thought.

'The older brother is out on bail at the moment,' Sita said, turning to her. 'But he was not in the house while we were there.'

Jay said nothing. The policewoman who came to see her every few days had already told her that.

'We saw one of your friends outside – Matt. I remember you telling me about him. He asked after you. He was very persistent. Why don't you call him?'

Jay gripped the edge of the table, so Sita wouldn't

notice her hands trembling. 'Did you . . .'

'No, of course not, Jay. We did not say a word. But he was so very worried about you. He said he has been calling you every day, but your phone goes straight to the answer machine. Neela said that he was one of your best friends – that he practically lived in the flat you had before you moved to No.42.'

Jay didn't reply. She went back up to her room and sat down, cross-legged, on the bed. She didn't switch her phone on immediately, just flipped it round and round in her hand, thinking. She thought about her mum and the kind of reception she had received at No.42. It must have been awful. Auntyji would have been mad as hell at her mum coming back for their stuff, after what they had accused her darling son of doing. She would have wanted blood.

Jay knew why her mum hadn't told her about the trip herself – because Jay would have accused her of using it to get back into her daughter's affection, which was how it would have come across, how Jay would have seen it. So her mum had left Sita to tell her. But at least her mum had finally stuck up for herself. That was a sign of her old mum emerging from the shadows – the mum she had missed, the one she needed. But why had it taken *this* to stop her being Vimala's doormat?

Then Jay's thoughts turned to Matt, and how much he meant to her. But he was part of her old life.

He wouldn't want her now. How could he? But how would she know for sure, unless she told him what had happened? And if he turned away from her – how could she live with that?

Jay knew she couldn't. Matt had been her rock, and if she turned to him now and he wasn't there, she would completely fall apart.

There were too many what ifs crowding her mind, spinning it round and round in circles, making her dizzy and getting her nowhere. Jay needed a distraction.

She picked up a book, but had only just started reading when there was a knock on the door. Sita popped her head into the room, looking pleased to see Jay doing something other than staring blankly into space or hiding under the bedcovers.

'Good book?' she asked.

'St Clare's.'

'One of Amala's favourites. I have saved them for my granddaughter, Priyanka,' Sita said. 'I will be out for a few hours this afternoon, Jay. Can I get you anything before I go?'

Jay shook her head.

'OK. I will see you later.'

Now that the house was empty, she could hear the ticking of the clock on her bedside table. Usually it was the only sound she found soothing – but not now, not today.

Thoughts were buzzing through her. She got off the bed and paced round the room, feeling wired. The need to do something was overwhelming. And what that was, was suddenly crystal clear.

CHAPTER 19

Jay got the rucksack from under the desk, hoping her Oyster card was in there, but it wasn't. She found her purse, and tipped it open. She had the grand sum of £3.57. She delved back into the rucksack, hoping that some change had fallen out of the hole in her purse. She found a couple of one-pound coins, some twenty-pence pieces and a few pennies. She had just over six pounds, more than enough for a round trip.

Someone had neatly folded her jeans and put them on the chair with her T-shirt. She slipped into them, shocked at how they now hung off her. She glanced in the mirror, an instinctive motion, and quickly drew back, but not before she'd caught sight of the haunted eyes of the stranger staring back.

She hunted round the room for her cap, pulled it over her head, and went downstairs, getting as far as the bottom step before sitting down, the sudden rush of energy draining away already. She had only left the house once since Sita had asked her in for a cup of tea, and that was to go to the SARC; the memory made her shudder. It was so tempting to forget her plan and crawl back up the stairs. The closed front door presented a barrier too hard to cross, and the world that lay on the other side of it made her tremble with fear.

Jay took her mobile out and pressed the 'Create Message' button. After adding Matt's name in the recipient's box, she hesitated.

What to say? How much to say? And how to say it?

It could only be the whole, blunt truth.

She used the word that she could still not say aloud. She didn't bother reading through what she had written because by the time she pressed send she could barely see a thing through her tears. The letters were blurred and her hands were shaking violently.

Jay didn't have to do anything else today. There was nothing from stopping her turning around and going back upstairs, or from going into the garden with a book and reading under the shade of the willow tree. Instead, she took a few deep breaths to steel herself and jerked the front door open, quickly, before she changed her mind. She patted her pocket to check the front door key was there. And she headed out – knowing where she wanted to end up, but with only a vague idea of how to get there.

Within a few minutes, Jay had reached a main road. She stood on the kerb, rocking on her heels, looking in both directions and wondering which one to take. Everything looked the same: row after row of houses and gardens. Jay went east, on the lookout for a bus stop. She spotted one not too far down, opposite a big supermarket set back from the main road.

Jay crossed the road and waited for the bus. It wasn't long in coming.

She didn't get off the bus until it had gone past her destination, which was safer because she would be less likely to bump into anyone she knew. Then she realized how stupid she was being – it was only two and everyone would still be in school. There was lots of time to kill, so she walked back to his house via a long, meandering route. She walked past the park, and then changed her mind and double backed to it. It was hot and she was tired already, so when Jay spotted an empty bench in the shade, she sank gratefully on to it.

The park was full of toddlers and pre-schoolers running around and screaming at the top of their voices, their mums pushing buggies or chatting to other mums, enjoying the warm, balmy day.

She would have far preferred grey, gloomy weather. It would have matched her mood. The park would have been empty too, and she wouldn't have had to suffer seeing other people living carefree, happy lives.

On the bus down, she had listened to the messages Matt had left, and read all the texts he'd sent that week. He obviously knew something was up. He wasn't stupid. He'd spoken to her mum and to Sita, and he knew something had happened on the night of the party. Had he guessed what?

The text she had sent him today wouldn't have come as a complete shock. Yet he hadn't bothered to send her a text back. She thought he would have by now. That's why she was here. How much longer should she wait? She almost jumped up and ran away then – back to the bus stop, back to Northwood, back to the safety of the pink room at Sita's, where she didn't have to think about anything or face anyone.

Jay left the park and began to walk towards Matt's house. She would give him a bit longer to respond. He was her best friend – he wouldn't abandon her, not now that he knew. He'd be there for her, the way he always had when things had gone wrong. He would wrap his arms round her and hold her close. The steady beating of his heart would soothe her, make her forget everything else.

Somewhere far behind her, she heard loud voices. Jay glanced back and saw the familiar flash of the brown and green Kingswell uniform. She quickened her pace, her heart thumping. School was out. She knew where to wait where she wouldn't be seen. There was a hedge along the bend in the road that afforded a clear view almost all the way back down to the park.

As the kids in uniforms approached, Jay began to feel increasingly nervous, but she resisted the temptation to bolt. She was sweating, her hands sticky and trembling. Maybe he hadn't read her text yet. Maybe he didn't know what to say. Maybe . . . maybe what? Was she just making excuses for him? Matt always checked his messages.

She couldn't run away though, not now. She needed him – and she wanted his help with . . . Deven.

Deven was out on bail, awaiting trial. He'd be out drinking with his mates, making the most of his freedom before the trial. The point was: he was at home and she knew where to find him. And she had to do something, before it was too late. She was counting on Matt to help her. Or would he try to talk her out of her madness? No amount of talking would change her mind about what she had to do.

The boys in Kingswell Secondary uniforms were less than fifty yards away now, but she couldn't make out their faces, and the harder she stared, the more blurred the faces became. Her heart beat faster. She was suddenly terrified that Matt would see her.

Was it him? She couldn't tell. There were three of them; one was tall with dark hair. It might be him. They drew level with her and went past. She let out the breath she had been holding in. It wasn't Matt. She had recognized them – Jack, Sanjay and Arthur; three boys from Year Eleven.

She should get out while the coast was clear. Even if the Year Eleven boys looked back now and saw her, they wouldn't recognize her. Jay took a cautious step and peeked down the road. A boy and a girl from Kingswell were heading her way. It was too late to make a run for it. She ducked back into the bushes as they approached.

The girl looked like Chloe, slender and blond, but Chloe didn't live up this way. She lived nearer the grocer's shop where Jay used to work. It couldn't be her. It had to be someone else.

The couple were talking animatedly and a giggle reached Jay's ears. She craned forward, parting the leaves for a better look. The girl punched the boy's arm playfully. She was walking really close to him, shoulders and hips touching now and then.

The boy must have said something nice, a compliment or something, because the girl's face lifted up to his with a smile. It was a bewitching smile – open and flirtatious, yet ever so slightly coy – and it made you want to smile back. Jay knew that smile. It was definitely Chloe.

By now, she also knew the other person was Matt. She could tell it was him by his careless saunter, by the way he turned his head when he spoke, and by the way he pushed back the lick of hair that always fell across his left eye. She watched them strolling leisurely up the road towards her. She suddenly felt dizzy and reached out and grasped at the hedge to steady herself. Matt's house was just up the road. They were going to his house. Both of them. Over the last year, Matt had only ever asked Jay back to his house to hang out.

So this was his reaction to her text. Matt, her best friend. Her boyfriend. The only person she trusted. The boy she had come here to confide in.

That's right, Matt – just move on to the next girl. And why not, when that girl was as gorgeous as Chloe was? As free and as normal as Chloe was?

'Gorgeous' was his word. Jay remembered the precise moment when he'd called Chloe that.

She pulled her cap further down on her head and shrank back into the bushes, willing herself to become smaller. She didn't want them to see her. Not now. Not ever.

Jay bit down hard on her lip to stifle a sob, and drew a drop of blood. It tasted like metal. She clamped her eyes shut and put her hands over her ears, but their laughter reached out to her, forcing her back, pushing her down to the hard ground. It taunted her – their thoughtless, uncaring laughter. She opened her eyes and saw Matt; he seemed to be looking directly at her. Their eyes seemed to lock, and, for a very brief moment, she thought he had seen her, the wild wide-eyed thing hidden in the undergrowth. Had she given herself away?

Chloe was chattering away, all brightness and light, her soft, silky hair swinging back and forth as she bobbed her head, drawing his eyes to her. But his eyes weren't looking at Chloe, they were looking over her shoulder. Jay shrank back. And then the moment passed, and they walked on. He hadn't seen her. He had been completely oblivious to the trembling girl cowering on the ground, hugging her knees, rocking gently, crying softly.

It had all been for nothing. For a brief moment, she couldn't even remember why she had bothered to come to Kingsbury. And then she remembered – her rage had carried her here. Her rage and the overwhelming need for revenge. She had come for help with her plan to hurt Deven.

That, and also because Sita had said Matt had been hanging around outside Primrose Avenue, desperate to see her. Sita had said he was 'very worried' about her. But he didn't look worried at all. He looked happy, without a care in the world. He'd moved on.

Jay felt as though the world had suddenly caved in on her.

CHAPTER 20

Her body folded in on itself as she lay on the dry, hardened earth, her knees drawn up against her chest, engulfed by an unbearable sense of loss, unable to make sense of how her life had gone so terribly wrong. Nothing could be put right – and her last chance had just walked away with another girl at his side.

A gentle breeze ruffled the leaves of the hedge, making the dappled rays of sunlight blink on and off, like a camera flash. She could not move, so she let it blind her until all she could see was a pure, brilliant white light, and she lost herself within it.

Jay was lost, lost in time.

Scenes from the past floated out of the bright light like a series of holograms, one after the other. She reached out but could not touch them. They flickered in and out of focus – and sometimes they were so tantalizingly close it felt as though if she took one little step, she would be able to touch them; go back through time and relive those memories, her happy memories.

Being carried on her dad's shoulders when she was about four, and held so high up, higher than everyone else. She was on top of the world and so safe because she knew he would never, ever let her fall. Getting tickled by him when she was six, begging him to stop but not wanting him to stop at the same time, and laughing so much she was crying. His face was so close. She put her hand out to touch it. But the smiling face and the eyes full of love and adoration faded into the white.

She cried out as he faded into the bright light.

Then it was her and her mum.

Jay lightly brushed her cheek with her fingertips as the memory of her mum's soothing touch reached out from the white. Jay had had flu, and her mum stayed with her night and day. Each time she opened her eyes her mum was there, watching over her with a reassuring smile, a flannel to soothe her brow, a sip of water to ease her throat. Then she too disappeared, fading into the white where Jay's father had gone. Jay screamed for her, but her fingers grasped nothing but air.

And then there was only her.

She knew what she had to do.

The key to the house was in her pocket, clenched within her fingers. She clutched it so tight it dug into her palm. The pain kept her focused. Jay strode purposefully up the road, only slowing her pace as she turned into Primrose Avenue. She gripped the key harder. She stopped at No.42. Her heart fluttered, making her falter mid-step – not because she had second thoughts, because she didn't. And not because she was afraid, because she wasn't. But because she didn't want to have to see the face that had tormented her, that woke her up every night screaming. She'd spent weeks trying to scrub that face from her memory, and here she was, walking willingly towards it. What if she froze when she saw him? What if he spoke to her? How would she deal with it?

If she returned tonight, while he slept – because she was sure *he* wasn't having any trouble sleeping – she wouldn't have to look at *that* face, see his eyes, when she took her revenge.

Should she return at night? Wake him as he had awoken her? Let him think it was a nightmare, then destroy him as he had destroyed her?

There was a chance he wasn't even at home.

Jay couldn't turn back now. She was too close. It

was revenge that had driven her here; revenge for what he had done to her, what he had taken from her. How was she meant to move on, until he had paid for it? He had been charged, but he was out on bail. Once the case went to court, he would probably be found guilty, but there was a chance he might not be. What if they decided he was innocent?

The STO, the specially trained officer who was assigned to Jay, had told her that he didn't have much of a case. The police had also interviewed the younger brother, she had said, and he had confirmed what had happened at the party, and that Jay had asked for a bolt on her door because she was afraid of his older brother. He had agreed to be a witness for the prosecution.

Jay knew that Aunty Vimala would never forgive Ash if he told the truth at trial. She would make his life a misery. By the time the trial came around, she would have made absolutely sure that he had recanted his statement. He wasn't tough enough to withstand her. And Uncle Balji? Jay didn't have a clue about where he stood, but Aunty V would make sure it was right behind her precious Deven. They would have hired the best lawyer money could buy.

And the STO had also warned Jay what Deven's lawyer might try to claim. That he thought she was older, because how was he to know any different? He didn't live in the house. He was away at uni. That she had consented, and that she liked rough sex.

And then he would be free. She couldn't live with that.

She turned into the drive, noting that neither her uncle's car nor Ash's car were there. But Deven's car was there, parked at a stupid angle, so that the others would be forced to park on the road. There was only one thing in Deven's mind and that was Deven and what he wanted. Nothing else mattered; no one else mattered. That's why she was there. She glanced at her watch. She had plenty of time. Jay had lived here for long enough to know that her uncle and aunt always went shopping in Southall on a Wednesday afternoon, and Ash didn't finish college till later.

Music was playing somewhere and, at first, Jay didn't know where it was coming from. She headed towards the side of the house where the wheelie bins were kept, and where the gate into the garden was never locked. She stepped around the bins, through the gate, and down the side of the house, ducking as she passed the window to the downstairs cloakroom. She stopped at the corner of the house and looked around the garden. The music was much louder here, but the garden was deserted. The upstairs windows were shut and so was the back door.

Her eyes travelled down to the narrow bank of windows at ground level, to her old room, and the gym. She knew where the music was coming from now – someone was in the gym.

Jay crept back round to the front of the house and pulled her key out. Her hands were shaking so much it took her for ever to slot the key into the lock and get the door open. She left the door ajar behind her, knowing she might have to get out fast, and because it made her feel less trapped. Already her chest was tightening with anxiety. The thought of having to descend the stairs to the cellar almost made her bolt for the front door.

She steeled herself and headed for the kitchen first, tiptoeing so her footsteps wouldn't give her away. She would need the element of surprise. The knife rack was full of sharpened knives – she knew exactly how sharp they were, because her mum sharpened them on the whetstone every week. Jay's job was to prep the vegetables when her mum was cooking, so she knew which knives were the sharpest, the best for fruit, for potatoes, for meat. She selected the right one, put it in her pocket, and headed back to the hallway.

At the top of the cellar stairs, she paused for a moment. Her heart was beating too fast, skittering wildly. The front door creaked, swaying with the breeze. It settled a little more ajar now, allowing a wider shaft of sunlight into the house. No one knew she was here. She could walk out now and no one would be any the wiser. Downstairs, the music played on, its beat relentless. Jay turned her back on the sunlight.

Her legs started shaking. She leaned against the wall for support. She'd only got as far as the third step down. She didn't think she'd find herself here ever again – not willingly. But here she was, back at the scene of a crime. A crime against her. Over the music, she heard him grunting loudly. Then a loud noise – he must have dropped a dumb-bell. Jay couldn't see his face, but it was already inside her head – and then the images of the night returned with a vengeance. A sob tore through her, but she stifled it. Not that he would have heard her from so far away. Tears sprang to her eyes as her hand tightened around the knife.

'Jay?'

Ash was standing at the top of the stairs. He came down the stairs quickly, crossing in front of her, blocking her way. The music was still pumping away in the cellar.

His eyes were drawn to the knife in her hand. 'I don't care if you kill him. But they will send you to prison, Jay. And that would be wrong. He's the one who needs locking up.'

Something inside her broke when he said that. Ash took her arm firmly and led her back into the hallway.

She let him, until the thought that Deven might not get convicted made her pull away from him. This was her only chance.

'And what if they find him innocent? You don't understand, Ash. What he did . . .'

'They won't! I'll make sure of that.'

'How? Your mum – she'll never let you testify.'

'She won't know until it's too late. Trust me, Jay. I won't let you down again. Now, give me the knife. Please. Before you get caught.'

'I can't,' she sobbed through her tears.

'They'll be back soon and Mum'll call the police if you're here. Please, you have to go. Give me the knife.'

'I want him to pay!'

'He will pay.'

'But –'

The music in the cellar stopped. They could hear Deven's voice, muffled, as he talked to someone on his phone.

'Please, Jay. Trust me on this. Give me the knife. I'll drive you wherever you want to go. Come on, Jay.' He started to pull her gently towards the front door.

He held her arm, guiding her as she stumbled. He took the knife from her, dropping it into a vase by the front door, before rushing her out to the car.

He started the engine. 'Where to?' he asked, taking off before she answered, anxious to get Jay away from the house as fast as possible.

'Northwood. 68 Brimmer Lane.'

He glanced nervously at her. 'I won't take you to the door. It's better that way.'

She nodded. 'Why are you helping me, Ash?'

'You know why, Jay. I should have put the bolt on your door. I shouldn't have waited.'

Jay slumped down in the seat, waves of exhaustion sweeping through her. She couldn't stop her hands from shaking, so she stuffed them under her legs. 'You weren't to know,' she said quietly.

'I'm his brother, Jay.' Ash was shaking his head. 'I never imagined that he would . . . I'm so sorry, Jay.'

Jay realized that Ash was crying silently. He brushed the tears away and pushed his glasses back up his nose.

'I wanted him to die,' Jay whispered. 'I wanted him to bleed to death, painfully, knowing it was me.' She held her trembling hands in front of her. If there had been a knife in her hands now, she would have dropped it.

'Is that really what you want? For it to be over that fast for him? He should rot in jail until he's a feeble old man and can't hurt anyone any more.'

She shook her head. 'There's no guarantee of that. They don't give people life for . . . for . . . rape.'

'He could get up to twenty-five years.'

'No. That won't happen.'

'You're only just fifteen, Jay. That makes him a paedophile and a rapist. He'll get a long sentence – and it'll be bad for him, once he's inside.'

They were nearing the supermarket not far from Sita's road. 'Pull into the car park here,' she told him.

Ash drove in, parked in a space, and turned the engine off. They sat in silence for a moment.

He turned to her. 'Forget about him, Jay. They'll lock him up and throw away the key.'

Dear, sweet Ash. He didn't have a clue. She couldn't stop the tears from falling now. 'Don't you watch the news? Everyone knows it doesn't work like that. He'll probably get three years in prison, with three meals a day, TV, and the gym. Nothing he doesn't have already. And with good behaviour, he'll be out after a year.'

'Seriously, Jay, you're wrong. I've been looking up the stats and he'll get at least eight years – maybe longer, maybe even life.'

'His friends will back up his story that I wanted to join their party.' The STO had told her that on her last visit to Jay. 'He'll spin it, paint a picture of lies about me, and the judge will believe his story.'

'Jay, wait, please –'

She opened the car door, wondering if she could make it back to Sita's house. The bright sunshine was suddenly unbearable, the heat too close. She ached.

'Will you be OK, Jay?'

'Ash . . .' she began – but in the end 'Thank you for helping me' was all she could say.

Jay shut the car door and waited until he had pulled out of the car park before setting off, her head down.

CHAPTER 21

The sun was still singing its song, trilling that summer was on its way, but Jay couldn't hear it, nor feel the sun's warmth on her face.

She was floundering, drowning in waves of self pity that surged and washed over her, dragging her under, inch by inch. She no longer had the will to fight.

Through tears, she punched out a blunt message to Matt, letting him know that she had seen him with Chloe. She wanted him to know that much – that she was no fool. She never wanted to see him again. She pressed send without a second thought.

Jay let herself into the house with the spare key Sita had given her. The house was empty, as empty and as desolate as she felt.

She went through to the kitchen and straight out the back door, the turmoil within her growing with every step. Strangely, Jay's turmoil focused her thoughts, allowing her to see – what was her dad's old phrase? – 'reality as it really was'.

And the reality was that she didn't have much of a life any more.

She tried very hard to see something . . . anything. It didn't even have to be particularly positive – just something that would help her think that maybe one day things would be OK, and that it was worth hanging around for that day to come, that it was worth struggling through the misery.

But she saw nothing. There was nothing to look forward to. Everything that was important to her was gone.

Her dad – was dead, and had been lost to her for three years.

Her mum – she couldn't bring herself to even look at her, never mind talk to her.

Home – she had no home; she was dependant on the kindness of strangers.

School – she could not face going back to Kingswell Secondary, or anywhere else in Kingsbury ever again.

Matt – he had given up on her and moved on.

And *he* was still alive, still breathing, still free.

She couldn't even do that much – not even with a knife in her hands.

What did that leave? Nothing. Some people were just plain unlucky, she decided, born at the wrong time, into the wrong family, in the wrong place by an accident of time and fate, coincidence and bad luck – and Jay was one of them.

Her feet led her down the garden path to the wooden cabin at the end. She was on autopilot.

Her mum would be far better off without her. She wouldn't have to worry about her any more. And she wouldn't have to suffer her daughter's bitter recriminations.

Jay stepped inside the wooden cabin and switched on the light. There was a musty earthiness to the cabin. She breathed in the powerful smell, submerging her senses in its moist warmth. She felt as though she was already deep underground. She was ready; ready to leave her body in the safety of the earth, so she could be set free and finally become a carefree spirit.

Without her daughter to worry and agonize over, her mum would finally get on with her own life. She would become a teacher and move somewhere nice. She had always wanted to live by the sea. Well, now she could move down to the south coast. She would be as free as Jay was going to be.

Jay was certain she was doing the right thing, and

with this certainty the burden began to lift from her shoulders.

She looked round the cabin, searching for the right tool for the job.

It was quite possible her mum might stay on with Sita. The two women had become very good friends in a short space of time. She had heard the soft murmur of their voices talking late into the night. They seemed to have so much to tell each other, so much to share. They were more like old friends who hadn't seen each other in years and years and had a lifetime of catching up to do. It was probably the best, and the strangest, thing to have come out of Jay's nightmare.

Sita's strength, her different Kenyan–Indian background, had all helped her mum. Jay had seen it. Neela was changing, and the changes were good. But they came too late for Jay.

Jay knew what she needed for the job, and she knew where to find it. She walked across to the wall, reached up and unhooked the lawnmower cable from the wall bracket. Sita wouldn't throw her mum out on to the streets. And her mum would never take advantage of Sita's kindness. She never took advantage of people; although she had let people take advantage of her. Neela would insist on paying her way at the very least. And the two women would keep each other company, and have even more to talk about late into the night.

As for Jay, she would have nothing to worry about any more either. There would be no more nightmares, no more rage, no terrible desire for revenge – and there would be no more guilt. No more pain. And nothing more to fear. Nothing to be afraid of. It was simple. It was easy.

It made utter sense.

She went outside, clutching her prize – a bright orange cable that would not split or snap or break, and which was strong enough to take anyone's weight. It was the perfect thing for the job.

She lifted her face up to the roof of the veranda and raised her arm to shield her eyes as the bright glare of the sun blinded her. She could not bear the sun now, could no longer suffer its scrutiny. The sun laid everything bare and you could hide nothing beneath its light. There was a time when she loved the sun, loved its warmth and light. Now she prayed for a darkness that was eternal.

The veranda was supported by four posts and a good strong beam that ran its whole length. The beam was perfect for what Jay had in mind. She positioned the chair directly underneath it, hoisted the coiled cable on to her shoulder, and climbed up.

She threaded one end of the cable through the space between the beam and the roof, and looped it over on itself. Beneath her, the old wooden fold-up chair wobbled and rocked dangerously. She caught hold of the beam to stop herself from falling off, and spaced her feet further apart to get a better balance. She didn't want to fall off the chair until she was ready.

Jay's fingers were hot and sweaty, and she was all thumbs, leaden and clumsy. Instead of getting cooler, the day was warming up for the evening. It was going to be a sweltering night. But she didn't think her mum and Sita would sit in the garden. Not tonight. Maybe not for a while.

She mopped her brow with her forearm and in the process accidentally brushed her baseball cap off. It landed on the ground near the chair. She almost got down to pick it up, because it helped keep the sun off her face while she worked. She couldn't bear the sunlight in her eyes – it made her head hurt, it made her see the faces of the people she loved, and she didn't want to see their faces now. They were a distraction and they might make her stop or change her mind, and she didn't want that. But she didn't bother picking her cap up – she knew that soon enough she would not need it. She had to keep her mind on the task and hurry. Her legs were beginning to tremble from the effort of balancing on the wobbly chair.

Jay turned her attention back to the job in hand, wondering how hard it could be to make a noose. It was turning out to be more difficult than she had anticipated. She tested it and realized with despair that she had done it all wrong. It wouldn't work like that. It would simply unravel when she put her head inside it and kicked the chair away. She'd land on the ground with a thump, and that wasn't part of the plan. She wanted to soar, soar high above the clouds.

She swore in frustration and started again from scratch. Quickly, she unthreaded the loops with her fumbling fingers; the orange cable pooled around her feet. She had to go much faster. The sun was getting hotter.

Sweat glistened on her brow, rolling down her face and into her eyes, making it hard to see. Her arms were aching from being held over her head and she was hot and shaky. Jay was tempted to get off the chair and lie down on the grass, just for a moment. A little moment out of the time she had left wouldn't matter. It wouldn't make a difference, because no one could stop her now. But she knew she couldn't do that – not even for a second. Her pain didn't matter now. Nothing mattered apart from getting the stupid knot right. And then she smiled. She was sure she was getting it right this time. She was almost there.

And then it was done. She was ready.

She paused before slipping her head inside it.

Did she have any second thoughts? No. She knew she was doing the right thing for herself, and for everyone else. She would no longer be a burden on her mum. She had wanted revenge – but even there she had failed. The courts would have to take care of that. He would lose his life, for a few years anyway. And afterwards, for what that was worth, he would be branded.

People would know what Deven had done. The whole Indian community would know. It was the biggest shame, the biggest *besti* that Aunty Vimala would have to live with. He might have to move away. But he would still be free.

Jay had lost her life for ever. He had taken everything away from her, and she knew she would never be free of the pain he'd caused. Never. The memory would always be there, no matter how hard she tried to bury it – there wasn't a corner of her mind deep enough or dark enough for it.

She used to be Jay. Soon she would be just a memory.

CHAPTER 22

'You won't find a socket for the lawnmower up there.'

Startled, Jay half-turned, the orange cable only half over her head. The chair rocked and swayed. She grabbed hold of the beam for support.

Sita was standing on the path, a basket with gardening gloves and implements hooked over her arm. Jay had no idea how long she'd been watching. The noose had required her full attention. She'd got there, but too late. She couldn't finish the job – not with an audience, not with Sita's eyes boring into her.

Or could she?

Sita wouldn't reach her in time. It would all be over in a couple of seconds.

But looking at the woman's face watching her, Jay

knew she couldn't do it. Sita looked startled, her eyes were wide, her lips a colourless line.

Oblivion would have to wait.

The cable slipped out of her fingers and slowly unravelled, twisting its way down to the ground where it pooled at the foot of the chair, leaving one looped knot hanging above her head. She looked up at it and then down at Sita's grim face. The knot suddenly looked so obscene. She quickly undid it and held the end of the cable in her hands. It was tough, much stronger than rope. It would have held.

Sita placed the basket on the table and carried on as though nothing out of the ordinary had happened. 'Besides, it rained last night, and the grass is too wet. We will go inside – it is far cooler there.' She held the chair firmly. 'Take care climbing down.'

Jay's head hurt. She stumbled off the chair and handed the end of the cable to Sita, who wound it up round her arm and stowed it away, back on its hook in the cabin. Jay heard the key turn, locking the shed door.

But still Sita did not talk about what had so very nearly happened in front of her.

'I did not know that you were a gardener too. I know your mother has green fingers. She told me she grew vegetables, herbs, tomatoes and even cucumbers and strawberries when you had a big garden. I wish I had the patience for such things. But it would make me happy if you looked after the garden for me. And your mother would be delighted.'

Jay clenched her hands tightly by her sides. She couldn't speak, because she was seething with an anger that made her want to scream and shout and rage at the whole world. She felt cheated. She had been so close. A couple of seconds more and it would have been over.

Sita was still talking. Jay wished she would shut up. How could she drone on about gardening after . . . after what she had just witnessed? Jay knew why. She was waiting for Neela to get back from work, so she could deal with it. Sita had had her fill of Jay's problems. 'You have to deal with her, Neela,' she'd say. 'She is *your* daughter.'

And what would her mum do? What would she say to Jay? Would she tell her off for being a bad girl, and tell her she mustn't do it again? Or might she simply hand her a length of rope and say, 'Get on with it then, if that's what you really want – I've had enough of you'?

Sita led the way back to the kitchen.

Jay retrieved her cap and grudgingly followed her. It was cooler inside the house, but Jay's skin still burned feverishly hot. The last thing she wanted to do was to sit down in the kitchen with Sita. All she wanted to do was to think about what to do next, because she didn't have a back-up plan. Suicide wasn't the kind of thing that required it: either you were dead, or you weren't. There was nothing in-between.

Jay made it across the kitchen, almost to the door, when Sita said, 'Sit down, Jay.'

'No, thanks. I'm going upstairs.'

'You will not! Sit down!' Sita snapped, her look so cold it froze the 'No' on Jay's tongue.

Sita didn't speak again until the tea was made. She sat down at the table and folded her arms. Jay steeled herself for the inevitable lecture. She was going to be told to stop being a stupid, selfish, thoughtless girl. Sita was just like the rest of them. That was all they saw. They didn't understand her pain, nor why she wanted to end it. But it made sense to Jay; it was the logical thing to do.

But Jay was caught off-guard when Sita began to talk. It wasn't the lecture she was expecting.

'I have never really spoken to you about my family. You know Amala is my daughter, and Priyanka is her daughter. But I have not spoken much of my son Anil or his wife Bhavna. They live in Brighton with their two boys,' Sita began. Her tone had softened, but her light-brown eyes were fixed intently on Jay.

Jay shook her head, not daring to speak. Sita had talked about Amala – she had married a Mauritian Indian and they lived in Mauritius. They came to stay for two weeks every year, and Sita went to them once a year. But she hadn't said much at all about Anil or Bhavna. She was probably going to tell her about how they had fallen out a long time ago, and how she'd regretted it ever since. Something designed to make Jay stop and think about what she was doing to herself and to her mum. Well, Jay had decided to get out from under everyone's feet – she'd find some other way, somewhere else, to finish the job. She didn't care what Sita was going to tell her. Nothing she could say was going to change her mind.

'She was raped. But her story –' Sita's voice broke for a moment.

She had said it bluntly and it had had the desired effect. Jay was stunned.

When she had collected herself, Sita began again. 'It is not something I find easy to talk about, because it is Bhavna's story. And it happened a long time ago.'

'I'm sorry. About Bhavna.'

'I will tell you a little of what happened to her – but maybe, one day, she will tell you herself.'

Jay shook her head. 'No. I don't need to hear her story.'

'Why? Because it will force you to see that you have every chance of a happy future? Because it will force you to pick yourself up and try to move forwards slowly? He did not kill you, Jay. You are here. You are alive.' Sita's voice dropped to a whisper. 'You have a chance at a happy life, Jay.

'My son and daughter-in-law backpacked around India for their honeymoon. They had just graduated and both had jobs lined up, but they had four months before they started work and neither of them had been to India. They were both brought up here. Bhavna's parents were also Kenyan–Indians.

'For the most part they had a wonderful time. Kerala and Goa were their favourite places. Then they went to Delhi, and from there they travelled to Agra to see the Taj Mahal. On the way back to Delhi they got lost.' Sita paused again, swallowing hard.

'There were four of them. They beat my son very badly. Bhavna was gang raped.' Tears were falling openly down Sita's face. 'They both survived. My first and only trip to India was while they were in hospital. I had to leave Amala here – she was doing her A Levels – while I went over, to bring Anil and Bhavna home. The following months were not easy. Anil's wounds healed, Bhavna's took time, and in many ways I felt I failed her. But Anil did not.' She turned to Jay. 'I have a good son.'

That was why Sita was so intent on helping her, Jay realized. She didn't intend to fail again.

'What happened in my garden – what very nearly happened,' Sita corrected herself, 'must never, ever happen again.'

Jay pulled away from her, but Sita took hold of her hand and held it hard.

There was such anger in her voice when she spoke again. 'And I will stay with you every minute of every day if that is what it takes. Do you understand me, Jay?'

Sita lapsed into silence.

Outside, the birds sang and the sun continued to shine. In the kitchen, the silence deepened.

CHAPTER 23

Jay didn't know she was crying, but her face was wet with tears. Stories like Bhavna's had been all over the news recently. Two of the women she had read about had died from internal injuries. Did Bhavna count herself lucky that she had survived? She had two children now, so maybe she did.

But Jay couldn't see how you went from victim to survivor. How do you trick your brain into thinking everything was going to be all right?

'Anil saw her through the worst moments. Counselling helped her too,' Sita said. 'And time.'

Jay had seen the counsellor twice and it hadn't done any good, as far as she could see. 'It hasn't helped me.'

'You've cancelled four sessions so far,' Sita reminded her.

Jay looked away. 'I – I don't know, Sita. I don't know if I can be normal again and do normal things. And I don't want – I don't want –'

'What don't you want?' Sita pressed gently.

'I really don't want to live,' Jay whispered.

'Oh, yes you do, Jay. You do – believe me.'

'I can't and I don't want to! And yes, I know I'm pathetic and selfish. But it's *my* choice if I want to live or die.'

Sita's mouth fell open.

Jay couldn't look at her. She went to the sink, poured herself a glass of water and drank it standing up at the sink. Her head was throbbing. She was too hot. She drained the glass and refilled it. And then turned to face Sita. 'You see, Sita, I'm a horrible person. I deserve to be dead. Don't try to save me any more.'

'You're letting him win, Jay,' Sita said.

Jay heard the words as she fled the kitchen. She ran upstairs, threw herself on to the bed, and buried her head in the pillow. She wished everyone would give up on her. She was a lost cause.

An hour passed, and at some point during that hour, Jay fell asleep. It was seven when she woke up. During the past week she had fallen asleep for hours at a time and had woken up shattered and drained as if she'd run a marathon in her sleep. Other times she'd woken suddenly from a nightmare, grabbing hold of the sides of the bed, the bed covers – anything – to stop herself from tumbling, head over heels, over the steep cliffs that in her mind's eye plunged into the dark abyss. The yawning black pit was always beneath her waiting to swallow her up, and she'd barely wake up in time to avoid it.

Was it death, that dark abyss, that yawning black pit?

And if she wanted it so much, then why was she trying to avoid it? Why didn't she let herself fall?

Jay lay in bed and thought about Sita's daughter-in-law Bhavna. Hadn't she wanted to kill the men who had done that to her? Hadn't she wanted to tear them apart with her bare hands?

Her counselling session a few days later went along the same lines as the previous two had: with the counsellor, Ann Derwent, trying her very best, and Jay unable to respond in anything beyond monosyllables. At the end of the session, Ann asked her if she wanted to see an Asian counsellor instead. 'They might have a better understanding of your background, your culture . . .'

That provoked a response from Jay. 'No! No way. Why would I want that?'

'Because I'm concerned that I'm not getting through to you and I wonder whether it's because I don't have the understanding an Asian counsellor might have about your background.'

'That doesn't mean they would understand better than you do.' And they definitely wouldn't understand her, Jay thought. They would judge her, instantly.

The counsellor smiled encouragingly. 'That's more than you have told me in the last,' she checked her watch, 'forty-five minutes.'

'If it's OK, I – I'd rather stay with you, please.'

'Then, if we are to work together, I will set some conditions. First, you attend every session. Second, I want you to promise you will try to respond to my questions. Third, I want you to tell me how you feel, so I don't have to spend the whole session guessing. Deal?'

Jay nodded. 'OK.'

'Same time on Monday then?'

Jay nodded. She left the counsellor's office and walked outside into the sunshine. It was another hot summery day, but the breeze was cool on her cheeks. She'd come alone – or rather, Sita had trusted Jay to go to the session alone. Her mum had nabbed her in the morning and, at first, Jay was petrified that Sita had told her about what had almost happened in the garden. But, to Jay's surprise, it had been Matt she wanted to talk about.

'I don't want to talk about him,' Jay said, turning to leave the dining room where her mum had been working on her college stuff.

'I saw him when we went to Primrose Avenue.'

'I know. Sita told me.'

'I asked him for his mobile number and gave him mine.'

Jay's heart dive-bombed. 'What? Why would you do that?'

'I only asked for his number in case of emergencies.' Her mother tried to gloss over it when she saw the consternation on Jay's face. 'Jaya, I promised him I would tell you this –'

'I don't want to know.'

'But he keeps calling me every day to ask after you. He wants to see you. I told him that when you were ready for visitors, you would let him know.' Her mum shook her head. 'But he is very persistent and very persuasive – and he is very upset.'

Yeah, so upset that he's spending all his time hanging out with Chloe, she thought bitterly.

'He asked me to tell you that it is very important you read his messages. I know he is your good friend, Jaya. But it is up to you. I have kept my promise to him, and I will not talk about it any more.'

Jay had left quickly. He didn't care as much as her mum thought he did, or he would have responded to her text the other day.

Jay couldn't face going back to the house yet. Sita had been watching her like a hawk. She wouldn't be surprised if she wasn't parked somewhere nearby, keeping an eye on her. Jay walked past a coffee shop, and at the last minute ducked inside. It was busy, but there was a table in the back corner that was free. She ordered a latte and sat down at the table. Not so long ago, the chair opposite her wouldn't have been empty. Matt would have been sat there, grinning at her, reaching across the table for her hand, making her laugh.

She shouldn't think about him. It only made her angry and sad.

Jay took her phone out of her pocket, wishing her mum hadn't brought Matt up earlier. Despite what she'd told her, Jay knew he didn't really want to speak to her, and how could she blame him? But . . . she missed him. She flipped her phone open and saw *12 messages received* flashing. Her heart skipped a beat. He still had that effect on her, despite his betrayal.

It was safer to ignore the texts and keep hold of that kernel of equilibrium she had today. One of the things the counsellor had said was that she had to be careful about the extremes of emotions she would feel. Like Miss Basma, she had also made her put her phone number into her mobile, in the first session.

But the other day, in the garden, the last thing on Jay's mind had been to call someone for help. She hadn't thought she needed it.

Jay didn't tell the counsellor anything about what she had tried to do – not about going to No.42, and not about the orange cable, and the noose that beckoned her. She'd heard about people being locked up in a mental ward if they were considered a danger to themselves – or others.

You were mad if you wanted to die.

Did that make Jay mad?

Her head sank into her hands. Did she really, really, really want to die? she asked herself.

She looked around at the faces of the people in the cafe, as they sipped their coffees, chatting. You couldn't tell what unhappiness or dark secret might exist in their lives.

Jay knew what she wanted. She wanted someone to make her feel unraped.

Jay sipped her now stone-cold latte. Her phone was on the table. Its insistent flashing meant she had received another text, and it was hard to ignore it. It would only stop when she opened the messages or turned the phone off. Her hands trembled. She reached a tentative finger towards the off button. She didn't have to read the messages now. They could wait until she was ready for them. Her finger hovered over the off button, but she pressed the sent messages button instead. She wanted to read the text she had sent Matt.

Jay scrolled down the list, but she couldn't find it. She went through the list again. It wasn't there. She was sure she had pressed send. She opened the drafts box – and there it was.

She hadn't sent it. She'd saved it as a draft . . .

He'd never received it. Matt didn't know what had happened the night of the party. He'd only got the text that she had sent when she was in the garden. When she had hit rock bottom. She had told him she had seen him and Chloe together, and that she hated him and never wanted to see him again.

She flipped through the messages he'd sent, one by one. All twelve said exactly the same thing.

Hey J, C is NOT my girlfriend, U R! U can't dump me with a txt message! Read about Deven in the local paper. Please, please, please call me, M xxxxxxxx PS. Remember we sealed our pact in blood!

Jay read it again, and again, and, slowly, the tiniest, smallest smile tugged at the corners of her mouth, catching her by surprise. Her eyes were full of tears, but she dabbed them away with a tissue. She needed to read his message again to make sure of what he was saying.

But there was nothing ambiguous in his message,

nothing that could be interpreted in a different way or misunderstood. She allowed herself a ghost of a smile. But it faded fast.

It could never work, she realized. How could it, when the orange cable was so tantalizingly close, the relief it would bring so near at hand?

And Matt obviously didn't know the whole story of what had happened at No.42 on the night of the party. He would dump her as soon as he found out. Any person in their right mind would.

She snapped her phone shut and shoved it deep into her pocket.

When she reached home, only Sita was in. Neela had gone to college and wouldn't be back until teatime. Jay went up to the pink room and lay down on the bed. When she woke up it was almost evening and she was hungry. She sat up in bed. The smell of food was drifting up the stairs and through the half-open door. Her stomach grumbled. She hadn't felt hungry for so long it was almost a strange sensation. Jay left her room and sat down on the top step, breathing in the cooking smells and listening to the soft hum of voices from the kitchen radio. Her mum would be back soon. She went back to the bedroom and stood in the middle of the room, wondering what to do. She didn't feel like lying down again. She picked out some clean clothes and a towel and ran a bath.

By the time she headed downstairs, Sita had turned the radio off and was watching a soap on TV. She probably wouldn't want to see Jay, after all the horrible things she'd said to her when they last spoke.

She stood uncertainly in the doorway to the living room. The last time she had spent any time in the room was that first Sunday night – in the spotlight of the police camera, surrounded by men and women in uniform. The room had looked completely different then. She was about to turn away and go back upstairs, when Sita saw her.

'Come and sit down, Jay,' she said. 'If you like,' she added gently.

Jay crossed the room and sat down on the armchair in the bay window. She looked out of the window on to the front garden. There was a birdfeeder hanging in the oak tree, which was popular with a family of robins living in the hedge opposite. They played tag, zipping out one by one for a quick nibble before flitting back to the safety of the nest.

'I'm sorry, Sita,' she said quietly.

Sita turned the volume down on the TV and faced her. 'I know you did not mean it, Jay. I am just relieved I was there.'

Sita was wearing a sleeveless red cotton dress, which ended just below her knees. It was still odd for Jay to see an older Indian woman in a dress, with bare legs. Her mum used to wear them when her dad was alive, but never at No.42. Aunty Vimala would have had an apoplectic fit.

'I'm lost,' Jay said simply. 'All I do is cry and be miserable and make everyone else miserable. It – it seemed like the right thing to do.'

'It's not. We can't imagine what you went through – what you're going through – but you must promise me you will never think of doing such a thing again. Promise me, Jay.'

Jay gulped hard. She opened her mouth to say the words, but they got stuck in her throat. 'I – I'll promise I'll try,' she stammered.

Sita nodded. 'That is a beginning. No one is expecting you to be back to your normal self – but if you begin very slowly, by taking small baby steps, one day you will run again.'

Jay doubted it very much. 'I tried, today. I went out. I saw the counsellor. I even went and had a coffee.' She couldn't tell Sita about how dead she felt on the inside.

'That's good, Jay. It is a start,' Sita carried on. 'You can always help me out around the house and the garden. Come down and watch television. Read, which you love doing anyway. Small steps.'

Maybe she was right, Jay thought. Maybe she could try. She had nothing to lose, nothing at all. She went back to staring at the robins and Sita turned her attention to *Coronation Street*, muttering a complaint about a ridiculous new plot line. 'Do you ever watch it?' she asked her.

'Only when Mum is back from work in time, but that was before – before we moved there.'

'I've been watching it for a very long time and I cannot break an old habit now.'

Sita filled her in on the latest developments, and Jay relaxed back into the chair and watched the rest of the programme with her. Other people's dramas seemed far less complicated than hers.

Her mum arrived as the credits were rolling. 'The bus was late again,' Neela said wearily.

'Don't worry, I have recorded it for you, and I have also cooked one of my specialities for dinner.'

If her mum was surprised to see Jay in the living room, she didn't show it. Jay cast a quick glance in her direction and gave her a small nod to say hello. She hoped that would be enough for her mum to leave her alone. Neela took a step towards her and then thought better of it and stopped, but she was smiling, happy to see her downstairs.

'How are you, *beti*?'

Jay couldn't bring herself to return the smile. 'Fine. Thanks.' She winced inwardly at her abrupt response, but it was as much as she could manage. She turned back to the screen where a deeply absorbing episode of *Eight for Dinner* captured her undivided attention.

The rest of the evening didn't go too badly and Jay managed to get through it. The fear that Sita would tell her mum about what had happened in the garden still felt real. She was sure she would tell her eventually – how could she not tell Neela about what her daughter had tried to do? That would come later, Jay supposed, after she'd gone to bed, in soft murmurs and whispers. She ate dinner with them at the kitchen table while Sita chatted to her mum about the current plot-line in *Corry*.

Sita's speciality was a south Indian dish – masala dosa. It was feathery light, the filling spicy and moreish. And, as long as Sita and her mum didn't try to include her in their conversation, it felt OK to be sitting with them. She found it hard to be in her mum's company. It was too painful – Jay actually felt an ache in her chest.

But her mum seemed to accept Jay's curt responses and the way she so obviously blanked her, without a word of complaint. Sita did raise an eyebrow at her occasionally, but Jay ignored her. At least she was sitting here with them. She had made an effort. Taken a baby step. That was what they wanted, wasn't it?

CHAPTER 24

Jay was anxious to get back to her room now. She helped tidy up after dinner and, just as she was about to leave the kitchen, her mum said, 'Jaya, I had a telephone call today.'

Jay didn't turn back, but she waited at the kitchen door for her mum to continue. She wasn't going to bring up Matt again, was she? After a year of practically banning her from seeing him, she had suddenly become his greatest supporter.

'It was your teacher, Miss Basma.'

Jay stepped back into the kitchen with such visible reluctance that Sita and her mum couldn't fail to notice it. Jay looked at her mum. She was twiddling her fingers nervously, her eyes not on Jay but on an invisible speck on the table. 'She's not actually one of my teachers. She's the school counsellor,' Jay said. Her tone was belligerent. She couldn't help it – it was the effect her mother had on her when she thought she was acting for the good of her daughter.

'I know that, Jaya. She was asking after you. She wanted to know how you are. She said she would like to come and visit you again.'

Jay's hackles rose. Just when she was trying really hard, her mum had to go and ruin it. She bet anything that Neela had responded with 'Yes, of course, Miss Basma, any time. Jaya is always at home' – taking the decision out of Jay's hands as usual. It was no more than she expected of her mum. 'I suppose you told her she could come over whenever she wanted, didn't you?' Jay said, with such hostility it shocked even her. 'So when is she coming? Because I need to make sure I'm not here. You're welcome to talk to her if you like!'

Sita ran her hands through her short grey hair in exasperation. 'Why do you have to jump to conclusions, Jay?' she began, but her mum laid a hand on Sita's arm.

'It's all right, Sita,' Neela said. She turned to Jay. There was no trace of anger when she spoke. 'No. I did not arrange a time, Jaya. I told her that I would ask you first.'

Jay shrugged. So her mum was trying too – but that didn't change the way Jay felt about her.

'What do you think, Jaya?'

Jay rubbed her temples. The constant offers of help and advice threatened to overwhelm her. But then, their fears were valid, she conceded. Only Sita knew how valid. Maybe it would just be easier to try harder, like Sita said, and then everyone might leave her alone. 'Yeah, OK. I don't see why she can't come here, if she wants to. I'm not going to school though.'

'Shall I give her a ring? Or –'

'No. I'll ring her myself.'

'As you wish, Jaya.'

Jay stood in the doorway for a few more minutes, but the two women had begun a conversation about the differences between north Indian food and south Indian food and seemed to have forgotten she was there. It could have been like that at No.42, with her mum and Aunty Vimala chatting and comparing recipes. But it never had.

Jay mumbled goodnight to them and they stopped talking long enough to bid her goodnight before resuming their conversation.

She went up to her room. She thought of it as hers now. It would be a wrench to leave it, but one day – and that day might come round sooner rather than later – she would have to do just that. She picked up her mobile phone and scrolled down to Miss Basma's number. She paused for a moment. If Jay's own specialist counsellor couldn't help her, what could Miss Basma do?

Jay knew that thousands of women had gone through what she had, but that fact wasn't helping her. How did they manage to feel normal again?

How did they manage to feel unraped?

She'd read somewhere that a woman was raped every half an hour in the UK. Jay remembered that, because she had a head full of facts and figures. The real number was probably far higher. So she wasn't alone. Thousands of women somehow managed to live with it.

One person she knew she would never be able to talk to was Sita's daughter-in-law, Bhavna. The mere thought of the two of them exchanging stories made her shudder violently.

It was half past nine and Jay knew she wouldn't be able to sleep yet. She considered going back downstairs to watch TV, but the thought of having to face her mother again stopped her. It was possible that Sita might have told Neela about the incident in the garden by now. Her mum would run through the whole gamut of emotions tonight and she would definitely head straight up the stairs and demand to talk to Jay. Jay simply wasn't ready for that.

No, she had to stay upstairs – ready to turn off the light and feign sleep as soon as she heard the soft footfall heading towards her room. She'd have to find a book to read to while away the time before she fell asleep.

Jay went out to the landing and stopped in front of the bookcase. She needed an easy read, something that kept the brain busy but didn't engage the mind. She selected a bestselling thriller. It was several years old now, but that didn't matter as she hadn't read it.

She slipped between the sheets and started reading. It was one of those formulaic detective novels, but it was set in North London and she liked coming across names of places she recognized. She'd guessed who'd done it by page fifty.

Jay would call Miss Basma tomorrow – just for a chat, she decided – and once she had decided that, the heavy cloud that had settled with such permanence on her brow felt a little lighter.

At some point she fell asleep, the book left open on the bed. Later, someone came in and put the book on the nightstand, turned off the bedside light and switched on the night light by the door. The sheets were straightened and smoothed down, and the window was left slightly ajar to keep the room cool. She was kissed ever so lightly on the forehead, but Jay didn't stir. She was in a deep, dreamless sleep.

It was the next day when Jay noticed her phone flashing again. She almost didn't bother reading the text, thinking Matt had set that same text on some kind of automatic send for the same time every day.

But she couldn't resist and flipped her phone open. It was from Ash.

Can you meet tomorrow? he asked. *It's important.*

She tapped out a text. *Yes. 1pm OK?* she replied.

He'd never sent her a text before. She wondered what was so important.

On Monday morning, Sita was in the house. She was arranging a vase of flowers, their colours bright and vibrant against the crisp, white linen top. Jay leaned towards the flowers and drank in the heady floral scent. The flowers at No.42 had all been plastic.

'Are you going out?' Sita asked her.

'I've got my appointment with the counsellor.'

Jay was afraid she might offer to take her to her counselling session. A light drizzle was falling outside, but the forecast was good for the rest of the day.

'I can go on my own,' she added quickly.

'It's no problem,' Sita said as Jay shrugged into her jacket in the hallway. 'I'll drop you off and pick you up later.'

'You have to let me do things on my own, Sita.'

'OK. But I will be a phone call away.'

Jay thanked her and hurried off, anxious to get the session over so she could meet Ash. She rang the buzzer for the counsellor's office and pushed open the door when the beep sounded.

'We made a deal, Jay,' Ann Derwent reminded her as soon as she walked in.

'I remember,' Jay said reluctantly. But despite herself, and despite the fact that they didn't talk about anything in particular, the session went better than usual. Jay's mum usually always came up in the session and today was no different. What *was* different, Jay noticed, was that her extreme anger towards Neela wasn't as overwhelming as it usually was. Something inside her chest clenched as she thought of her mum kneeling down among the filth of the gym room and retrieving her locket. She had returned it to her a few days ago – repaired.

'Same time on Wednesday?' Ann asked.

'Yes. Thanks.'

'And thank you, Jay.'

Jay guessed she thought the session had gone better too. She walked down to the coffee shop and took her latte to the table at the back to wait. She was fifteen minutes early, so she got her book out of her bag to read. Ash arrived exactly at one o'clock. He spotted her at the back and came straight towards her. She stood up to say hello and he awkwardly tried to hug her, mumbling 'Sorry' as he bumped the table and spilled half her coffee.

His clumsiness made Jay smile. She hoped Ash would never change.

'I'll get you another one,' he offered, dashing off to the counter.

As soon as he set her fresh latte and his cappuccino down she asked, 'What was so important?', unable to wait any longer.

'You didn't tell anyone about being at the house, did you? Because you mustn't. OK?'

Jay shook her head. A sense of foreboding came over her. 'Why?'

'I just wanted to make sure.'

'Is that all?' She didn't wait for him to reply, but carried on, 'Why? Are you having second thoughts about telling the truth?' She could feel her voice rising, the anger that always simmered just below the surface suddenly bubbling up. 'Oh my God!' she exclaimed, as realization dawned. 'He got to you, didn't he? Did you tell him I was there? I bet your mum got it out of you. So they're going to use it against me. I should have killed him when I had the chance!' Her voice cracked with emotion. She pushed away from the table to leave, but he caught hold of her hand.

'For God's sake, Jay, will you sit down and let me finish? Please?'

She sat down, perching on the edge of her chair, her latte untouched. Ash took his glasses off and gave them a quick polish, before setting them on his nose.

That was his nervous habit; Jay knew it well. Why

had he bothered to meet her, if it was only to tell her about his cold feet?

'I didn't tell anybody – not my mum, and certainly not Deven. And there is no way in hell that I won't still be testifying for you, so relax about that. I've already given a sworn statement to the police. I'll be in court for you, Jay.'

She exhaled slowly and settled back into her chair.

He leaned forward, glancing around to make sure he wouldn't be overheard. 'They don't know I know this, but I heard Deven talking to one of his uni mates. It looks as though someone else has come forward, from uni, and accused Deven of – of the same thing. It happened a few months ago apparently, but she was too scared to tell the police. She told a friend. Anyway, the police know about it now. Just thought I should let you know.'

Jay didn't know what to say.

'Don't let on you know, OK?'

She shook her head. 'I won't,' she whispered. The tears flowed without warning. For once Ash didn't hesitate. He came round the table and put his arms round her.

'You'll be all right, Jay. Just don't do anything stupid, like come to the house again. I'm with you on this, Jay. You can trust me.'

'Thanks, Ash.'

He took his seat opposite her again. 'No problem. Just ring or text if you need anything – a lift somewhere, or, you know, anything.'

A week passed. Jay had a routine of sorts that she followed: she got up, showered, got dressed, then breakfast, lunch, and dinner punctuated the day, but she tried to stretch out each activity to minimize the empty hours in between. Those dangerous on-her-own thinking hours that left her feeling wretched and desolate.

The night-time hours were still the hardest. Sleep came intermittently, the nightmares no less terrifying. The slightest sound would wake her, and she would clutch the duvet until she was sure there was no one standing on the landing outside her door. Knowing that it was all in her head – the noises, the fear, and the panic they induced in her – didn't help. She didn't know how to fight it.

Sita was always popping out, but never for very long. She didn't make it obvious, but Jay knew she was watching her. The shed door remained locked, cutting off access to the orange cable, and Jay began to get better at blanking out all the things that made her die a little on the inside: how things with Matt could never be the same again. How Deven had destroyed her. How she couldn't love her mum. It was the only way to get through the long hours of the day.

And not a word of what had happened in the garden that Friday afternoon had been mentioned – not by Sita, and not by her mum. Jay didn't have the guts to ask Sita whether she'd told Neela, but she knew she didn't want her to know. Her mum would think it was a cry for help.

But it wasn't.

Over the last few days, Jay had thought about it a lot. At that point in time it hadn't been a cry for help. It was Jay's attempt to resolve things. Once and for all. If it hadn't been for Sita, she would have been dead now.

Jay had been given a reprieve. If her counsellor knew about it, she would have said it was a second chance at life – except it didn't feel like a second chance, because there had been no epiphany, no life-affirming moment that made her want to carry on struggling through the pain and misery. She was still just as pathetic. She just tried not to think about it.

The difference was, the heaviness that lay like a weight on her – made it hard to open her eyes, to drag herself down the stairs, to talk to people, to gaze at the sunshine – that heaviness had lifted, or at least, it didn't feel as heavy.

Was that progress? Jay wondered.

CHAPTER 25

On Saturday morning, there was a knock on Jay's bedroom door. She groaned and buried her head under the pillow. It was early. Her mum was at college, so at least it wasn't her at the door.

'Are you awake, Jay?' Sita called from the other side of the door.

Jay rubbed her sleepy eyes. 'Mm, almost.'

'Good.' Sita came in, dressed in jeans and a short sleeved shirt. 'I've brought you up a cup of tea. Come and have breakfast when you're dressed, but please do not be long.' She placed the mug on a coaster on the bedside table. 'It is going to be very hot today, but there is shade under the willow where we can do the pots.'

'Pots?'

'Yes, I need your help with them.'

Sita left the room and Jay stretched and yawned. It was all part of Sita's mission to get her out and about – to keep her busy so she didn't have time to think about anything else.

Jay had been dragged to the library, which she'd ended up joining, and been asked to go to the supermarket a couple of times. Sita had made even bigger plans for the following week, one of which was to take Jay to the hairdressers to fix her hack job.

Jay thought she had provided a new-found purpose to Sita's lonely life, until they'd stopped at the hospital on the way to the library. Everyone there knew Sita and wanted to know if she hadn't been well the past few weeks, because they hadn't seen her. It made Jay suddenly realize how much Sita was putting herself out.

Sita wasn't lonely. She was just doing as much as she possibly could not to fail Jay.

Jay took a few sips of tea and got dressed. They were out of the house by nine-thirty and back by eleven, with the car boot and the back seat bursting with colour. Jay had surprised Sita, and herself, with her knowledge of flowers – most of it gleaned while spending long hours in her old garden reading as her mum pottered about around her.

After an hour of very hot and sticky work, the plants had been potted and placed according to the exact specifications left by Jay's mum. They sat down on the rickety fold-up chairs in the shade of the veranda, sipping cold lemonade. Sprigs of mint floated on the top. It was quiet and peaceful. A gentle breeze kissed Jay's skin as it brushed past her. She wanted the moment to go on and on and never end. She wanted to bring a book down to the garden and lie down under the shade of the willow tree forever.

Sita had shut her eyes and tilted her head back. Jay thought she might have nodded off, until she spoke.

'I think we can leave the lawn for one more week before it needs to be cut. Do you agree with me, Jay?'

Jay picked at the soil trapped beneath her fingernails. She didn't look at the beam above her head. The beam she had spent an afternoon wrapping an orange cable round. She wasn't sure how it would make her feel.

'I don't know,' she replied. Her voice was so small it was barely audible.

Another week. Jay knew what Sita was asking her, and she thought that if every day was like this then maybe she could manage it. Maybe. Being alone was where the danger lay. It was when she was alone that the thoughts crowded in – clamouring to be heard, demanding action. And they weren't good thoughts.

'I'm not sure. Maybe.'

'Good.' Sita sighed and closed her eyes and leaned back in the chair.

'Sita, did you tell my mum about – you know, what happened that Friday?'

'I thought about it, but I decided not to, not yet. Perhaps I never will. I may leave it up to you to tell her, or not.'

Tears pricked the corner of Jay's eyes. 'Thank you.'

'Right – lunchtime, then,' Sita said. 'Hungry?'

'Um, yes, I am a bit.'

In the kitchen, Sita took things out of the fridge to make sandwiches, but Jay took over, insisting on making them.

'You seem not so despondent these last few days, Jay,' Sita remarked.

'How can you tell?'

Sita turned her long neck and looked at Jay, her dark eyebrows raised. 'Because you have not spent much time hiding away in your room this week. Not like before.'

'There are wobbly moments though. Times when I think I – I might fall,' Jay admitted.

Sita put her arm round Jay's shoulder and squeezed. 'And that is normal. That is when you find someone to talk to. It does not matter who it is – so long as it's not just you and that voice in your head.'

Which one? Jay wondered. She had two voices in

her head. She cut the brown loaf into slices and got the butter dish. Once those voices got going, there was never room for anyone else.

'Listen, Jay,' Sita began hesitantly, 'I have been discussing something with your mother. What would you think about living here on a more permanent basis?'

'Sorry?' She was sure she'd misheard Sita.

'Neela will not make any decision without discussing it with you first. I have two rooms that I would rent to you and your mother. I was thinking of taking in a lodger at some point anyway. This makes more sense to me.'

'But –'

Sita raised her hand, warding off the *Buts*. 'No, I'm not going to listen to you. I'm going to tell you what I want you to do, and I want *you* to listen to *me*.'

Jay knew where this was going – the only place it could go.

'Your mother is afraid to even breathe around you. So I want you to start talking to her – from today.'

This was too much for Jay to absorb. Sita had offered them a home – it was the best thing that could have happened. But . . . it was too much, too generous. And then there was the condition that she'd imposed. Jay could still barely bring herself to look at her mum, much less talk to her.

'You don't have to do this for us, Sita – just because you feel sorry for us.'

'That is exactly what Neela said too. I will be honest with you, Jay. I like you, and I like your mother. I have two spare rooms. It is very simple.'

Jay buttered the bread quickly. A lump had formed in her throat. It was hard to comprehend that someone actually liked her, especially when she had done nothing to deserve it.

'I've caused you nothing but problems. How can you still want to have me around? How can you like me after – after . . .'

'Well, when you say it that way, I do wonder!' Sita laughed. 'But I do,' she continued seriously. 'I do want you here. It can be for as little or as long as you want, of course. But you will have to talk to your mother first,' she said adamantly.

Jay arranged the cheese, tomatoes and cucumber inside the bread and cut the sandwiches in half. Was her mother really afraid around her? Jay couldn't talk to Neela without biting her head off – and the longer it went on, the harder it was to do something about it.

She poured two glasses of juice and sat down. 'It's not easy.'

'Do not blame her, Jay. What happened was a terrible crime. But she did not commit it.'

'No. I'm not blaming her.' A slice of cucumber fell

out of Jay's sandwich and she pushed it round her plate, avoiding Sita's eyes.

'Oh, I think you are, Jay,' Sita replied. 'You are making her suffer, and it is not right.'

'I'm not doing it on purpose. I haven't been thinking about *her* in all this. It's not about her, is it? She wasn't abandoned in a cellar and raped! It wouldn't have happened if she'd – if she'd been there for me.' There, she had said it. Out loud.

'It wasn't her fault, and deep down I think you know that is true.'

'She . . .' But Jay couldn't finish.

'She is hurting, Jay. You are her baby, her whole world. You are everything to her. Do you really not care?'

Jay took a large, angry bite out of her sandwich. She couldn't reply, with her mouth full, but the food suddenly tasted awful. She swallowed it with a gulp of juice.

'Jay?'

'Of course I care!'

'Then please think about what I have said.'

Jay said nothing. She knew that if she replied she would say something she would regret. They finished their lunch in silence. Afterwards Jay asked, 'Is it OK if I go upstairs?'

'Yes,' Sita replied. 'But please think carefully about

what I have asked you,' she added. 'It is important.'

Jay did want to be able to love her mum the way she used to. She wanted it all to be the way it used to be. But it wasn't.

Was it possible to fix something so broken?

Back in the pink room, Jay shut the door and lay down on the bed. She faced the wall and stared aimlessly at the pattern of pink roses floating across creamy skies. She didn't want to think about the future, or her mum, or the cause of all their problems, but it was all she could think about.

She got off the bed and sat down at the desk. Sita was a truly kind and generous person – and the only other person Jay knew who was like that was her own mum.

Neela was strong, tougher than any woman she knew – she hadn't even had time to grieve after Jay's dad had died. She'd been too busy trying to put Jay back together – and yes, the flat above the grocer's had been poky, but she'd saved them from ending up on some rough council estate, scraping a living off benefits. Everything Neela had done was done to better their lives, including the move to Primrose Avenue. She wasn't to know what might happen there; what did happen.

What if she was to lose her mum through this?

What would Jay have left? Nothing. Nothing at all.

With a terrible ache in her heart, she suddenly realized how much she missed her, how much she loved her, and how she couldn't bear it if her mum never spoke to her again.

But would her mum still love her in the same way? Could she? And how soul-destroying would it be to discover she couldn't?

Sometimes, when she closed her eyes, Jay could see the luminous orange cable swinging in the sun. The noose still invited her in, tempting her with its promise of making all her insurmountable problems disappear. Today, the problems seemed no less insurmountable, no less overwhelming – yet, somehow, the noose wasn't as tempting.

Maybe it was because of Sita's offer. Or maybe it was because Jay had finally realized that losing one parent had been bad enough.

And she couldn't let *him* win. She hadn't seen it that way before Sita had said it. Now she knew better. She must never let him win. Ever.

The roller coaster was beginning to slow down. All Jay had to do now was to find her feet, steady them – and then she could get her life back. How hard could it be?

CHAPTER 26

Sita was in the kitchen, cooking the evening meal. She was slicing vegetables at the counter, her back to the kitchen door and the radio on in the background.

'Sita?' Jay asked. She didn't hear her. 'Sita?' Jay repeated a little louder.

Sita turned and smiled at her. Jay crossed the space quickly and threw her arms around her. 'I'm sorry, really sorry. Please don't ever tell my mum about – about what almost happened. Please.'

Sita held her in her arms. 'I won't say a word.' She cupped Jay's face in her hands. 'But promise me you will talk to someone if you ever feel that low again.'

'I promise,' she replied, and she meant it this time.

'And what about your mother?'

Jay pulled away and looked at Sita. 'I'm going to try. Really hard.'

Sita smiled. 'Good. The first few steps will be the hardest. Take them quickly to get them out of the way.'

'I was really, really lucky to have bumped into you. I don't know what would have happened if – if you hadn't been there.'

'Shush, Jay. We will not think about that now,' Sita said. Her brown eyes were brimming with tears. 'I must start the dinner before it gets late.' She turned away and sniffed.

'What are you making?'

'Something vegetarian.'

'You know my mum doesn't expect you to cook for us every day, don't you?'

Sita glanced up. 'And you know that because you have had a conversation with her recently?' she enquired.

Jay shrugged. 'No, not recently. Sorry. '

'Well, I'm following Neela's recipe for cauliflower and potato curry and tarka dhal.'

Jay smiled. The last time she had cooked that meal was in the flat above the greengrocer's. The phone rang and when Sita answered it, Jay realized it was her daughter calling from Mauritius. Sita took the phone into the living room. When she emerged some time later, Jay had finished cooking and was watering the pots in the garden. Sita came up behind her and hugged her, before going back inside.

Jay came back in just as her mum walked into the kitchen.

Neela set her bag down. 'It smells good, Sita. I hope my writing wasn't too hard to read.'

'Jay cooked dinner for us tonight,' Sita replied. 'She is such a good cook.'

'Yes, she is. She's had lots of practice.' Her mum turned to her and very tentatively said, 'Hello, Jaya. How are you?'

'Hi, Mum.' And then she added, 'I'm OK. How are you?' It was more than she had said to her mum in ages, and she didn't avoid looking at her this time either. She looked, and she saw how much she had aged. And it made her feel bad. She wanted to throw her arms around her mother and hug her and tell her how sorry she was. But she couldn't do it. She wrapped her arms around herself instead and half-smiled at her mum, hoping it didn't look too much like a grimace.

How can you forget how to smile? Wasn't it like riding a bike – once learned, never forgotten?

Throughout dinner, Jay tried to say something to her mum – anything, even the mundane day-to-day things, like 'can you pass me the salt' – but it was hard. Her mouth would dry up and the words would get stuck in her throat. She forced them out, but it left her feeling utterly hopeless. She began to panic that Sita would leave her alone with her mum after dinner, and she was afraid she would either clam up – or worse, end up being nasty to her.

It was easier to go back up to her room and read a book than try to say sorry to the person she loved most in the world.

Just as Jay feared, Sita left the kitchen after dinner, with the words, 'Just going to watch some TV.' She gave Jay one of her meaningful looks as she left the room.

Jay almost bolted out after her. It was stupid being this scared of her mum, of her reaction, but she was. She sat at the table, fiddling with her fingers, tugging at the ends of her hair, trying to stay calm. What if she said sorry and her mum didn't even look round? What if she said sorry and her mum said it was OK, but didn't even look at her?

Neela started washing up at the sink. Her shoulders were slightly stooped, her hair tied in a neat bun at the nape of her neck. She looked twenty years older than she was – older than Sita. Matt used to think her mum was beautiful, and he would joke that she would find someone eventually and remarry. He had no idea her mum was traditional in that way and would be appalled at the mere thought of marrying again.

But even without the glamorous clothes and coiffed

hair, the glitter and the gold dust, her mum was still the most beautiful woman in the world.

And Jay realized she must have finally turned a corner.

'Mummy?' she said, finally finding her voice. 'Mummy, I'm – I'm sorry.' She wanted to say 'I'm sorry for shouting at you, sorry for saying those horrible things. Sorry for everything. I didn't mean any of it. I know it wasn't your fault' . . . but the words wouldn't come out.

At the kitchen sink, her mum's shoulders were shaking and Jay knew she was crying.

Her mother wiped her hands on the tea towel and turned to her. 'Come here.' She wrapped her arms around her and held her tight. They stayed like that for a long time, just holding each other.

And then they were both crying, but it was a good kind of crying because there was someone to hold you.

Later, they sat down at the table and held hands and talked for a long time. They talked about No.42, and they talked about *him*, although neither of them could bring themselves to utter his name. They talked about what would happen, the trial, everything. And then they talked about the future, and Jay told her mum that she wanted to go back to school, but that she would never go back to Kingswell. She told her lots of other things, too, and her mum listened to her.

Jay didn't tell her mum about what had almost happened in the garden. Over a week had passed since then, but sitting with her mum now, it felt further away. Jay was hoping that, eventually, the memory of it would fade for her – she knew now that she didn't want it to be part of her future. But if she told her mum about it, it would always be there – another burden her mum would carry around in her heart.

Jay also made no mention of going to No.42 with the intention of taking revenge. That secret would remain between her and Ash.

'One more thing, Jaya,' her mum said. 'Your friend, Matt.'

Jay looked down at her hands. 'There's nothing to say.'

'I was wrong to stop you from seeing him, wrong to force so many changes upon you when we moved to number forty-two.'

Jay shrugged. 'It's in the past now, Mum. I don't want to talk about that place any more.'

Her mother leaned over and clasped her hands in her own. 'And we will not. But your friend. I . . . I know you were very close.'

Was her mum trying to ask her how close they were? 'Mum, I –' Jay began, but her mother interrupted her.

'Wait, please, Jaya, let me finish. All I wanted to say is that I will not stand in your way. I know you are very different to the way I was at your age – which is understandable, because you live in a different world to the one I grew up in. So as long as you are sensible, and – and . . .'

Jay grimaced inwardly. Her mum was trying to say it was OK for her to see Matt, even as a boyfriend – but she was having problems saying it in a way that was discreet, without mentioning what a relationship with a boy might imply, and in a way that wouldn't upset Jay. 'It's OK, Mum. I know what you're getting at. You don't have to worry. I'm not going to see him. Or anyone else, for that matter.'

'But you must! It would be a terrible shame to lose such a good friendship.'

'What?' Jay said, taken aback by her mum's insistence.

'Think about it, Jaya. If it would make you happy to see him, then see him. If you feel it would be too upsetting, then don't.'

Jay bit her lip, tears welling in her eyes. 'He wouldn't – I couldn't –'

'He calls me every day to ask after you. He has sent you many texts, but you do not respond. But he is a loyal friend, and he is waiting, Jaya. It is up to you.'

Jay went upstairs feeling light-headed. Was this happiness? Or relief? She wasn't sure, but it was definitely a special high. The kind of moment that Sita had said should be celebrated. She hadn't felt this way for a long time. Matt used to make her feel like this.

Jay didn't think of herself as a survivor, but she was surviving, for now. The rest was up to her, wasn't it? 'You can do anything you want to do, be anything you want to be,' her dad used to tell her. 'But don't forget to be true to yourself. You are Jayalakshmi Sharma. Don't ever forget who you are'.

She picked up her phone – it was flashing with new messages. Her heart beat hard as she flipped the phone open.

It was a new message. From Matt.

Call me. PLEASE. I miss you xxxx

Would it ever be OK between them? she wondered. Did she have the courage to call him? Maybe even to see him?

CHAPTER 27

Jay was back in the coffee shop, waiting. She crossed her legs and then uncrossed them. Checked her phone and put it down. Picked it up and scrolled through the messages, rereading them, and set the phone down again.

She pulled her cap further down her head, hiding as much of her hair as she could. Her eyes constantly flitted between the door to the cafe and her phone. She knew she shouldn't have arrived so early. If anything, she should have got here late. She hadn't thought it through, hadn't thought how nervous she would get waiting. She hadn't even brought a book with her to distract her, but it wouldn't have helped. She wouldn't have been able to read a single line.

The door opened and her eyes swung up instantly. But it was a middle-aged couple. She almost jumped up then and legged it out of the cafe – back to the pink room at Sita's, where she was in control, where she could hide and no one would disturb her. Where she didn't have to face anyone.

'Hey, Jay.'

Somehow he was standing right in front of her. She hadn't noticed the door opening, or seen him approaching. She tried to smile, but the smile wobbled. Tears welled in her eyes. He looked just the same; same tousled dark hair, same grin, same deep brown eyes, which hadn't shifted from her face. 'Hey, Matt.'

He came round the table to her, took her arms and raised her up, so she was standing in front of him. 'Come here,' he said, and wrapped his arms around her. And she let him.

Jay's cap fell off on to the floor and he bent down to pick it up. 'Whoa, radical haircut,' he said. He ran his fingers through the ends, his hand settling on her cheek. 'It suits you.'

The next evening, after dinner, her mum took her arm and led her out into the garden. They strolled arm in arm, the evening air cooler now that the sun had begun to set. Vibrant pink and orange beacons soared across the fading blue pastel sky. Jay showed off the pots she had planted with Sita. The flowers looked beautiful in the early evening light.

'I knew you took something from me – we can make anything grow,' her mum said proudly, squeezing her close.

'I hope Sita doesn't ask me to try to grow vegetables or anything, though. That's your thing.'

'And that depends on whether you have been thinking about what we talked about yesterday. Do you want to stay here? Or should we try on our own again?'

'Does Sita really want us here, Mum?'

'Yes, I think so. It would be very different to Primrose Avenue, Jaya. And we will be paying rent here, but it will be manageable, for both of us.'

'As long as you don't intend to skive off your teaching training course any more.'

'And as long as you decide to go back to school!' her mum retorted. 'A new school. It will not be easy for you, Jaya. You are halfway through the GCSE course.'

'I'll manage, Mum.' Jay thought she could cope with anything now – as long as it didn't involve going back to anywhere near Kingsbury. 'St Monty's has a scholarship for A Levels. So I need to get my act together soon.'

The sun disappeared and the sky quickly darkened to a cloudless midnight-blue. The stars were coming out, twinkling pinpoints of light. The final remnants of the heat of the day were blown away by a sudden cool breeze. Jay shivered.

'Let us go in, Jaya,' Neela said, pulling her cardigan around her. 'I think it is time to tell Sita what we have decided.'

Jay walked into the living room with her mum, their hands clasped tightly within each other's. Sita was immersed in a book, the television on low in the background. She looked up at them expectantly. 'Well?' she said, her tone was hopeful, her eyes smiling at the sight of this estranged mother and daughter holding hands.

'We have talked and talked.' Neela smiled at Jay and gave her hand an extra hard squeeze before turning back to Sita. 'And we have both decided that we would very much like to accept your kind offer. We would be so very, very happy to stay here with you, Sita. Thank you.'

Sita was beaming, with tears glistening on her cheeks. She got up and hugged them both. 'I am very happy.' She sniffed loudly.

Jay's mum was wiping away her own tears with an embarrassed laugh. 'We could never repay your kindness.'

'Not in a million years!' Jay said with feeling. Her voice caught in her throat and she felt the familiar prick of tears in her eyes. But it was the promise of hope, the promise of happiness that made the tears trickle down her face. At that moment, with these two women at her side, she felt loved and wanted, and all else paled. There was a future.

'Jay, you must change your room to exactly the way you would like it. It is your room now. Do whatever you want to it to make it feel yours. Priyanka only comes here once a year for a couple of weeks, so you must not think you have to keep it as it is for her.'

Jay was horrified. 'Oh, no, I couldn't do that, Sita!'

Sita gave her one of her looks. 'Oh yes you can. This is a new start for you.'

Jay understood what Sita was getting at, but she wasn't ready for that kind of change yet herself. The pink room had been her haven, her sanctuary, for the last few weeks. She remembered exactly how she'd felt when she'd first seen it.

'Actually, Sita, I love the room just the way it is.'

Sita didn't look convinced. 'Are you sure? We can at least look at some colour testers tomorrow in case there is anything you like better.'

Jay knew there wouldn't be anything better.

'And I will help you paint it,' her mum said, squeezing her hand.

Jay thought about it for a minute. Not everything was better for a lick of paint. She looked from her mum to Sita and, smiling at them both, said, 'Nope. I think I'll keep it pink.'

The front door bell chimed.

Sita got up to answer it. 'You don't need to make any decisions on it yet, Jay.' She returned a minute later. There was a surprised expression on her face. 'You have a visitor, Jay. I've asked him to wait outside for a moment. Do you want to see him? I can tell him you're busy, if you don't feel up to it.'

Jay glanced nervously at her mum. Her mum gave her a nudge, smiling. 'Go. Go and talk to your friend.'

Jay knew who it was. She'd told him the address when they were sitting in the cafe. They'd sat there for hours yesterday. Four lattes and three hours later, she'd sent him home, and he'd gone, but reluctantly, promising he'd visit her soon.

'Hey.' His tall frame filled the doorway, and in his arms he held a bubble-wrapped package, which got in the way as he tried to hug her.

Jay heard the living-room door close. Her mum and Sita were giving her privacy, but she still felt awkward.

'Shall I come in?' Matt asked her as she dithered on the front door step.

'God, sorry, yes. Come in.'

'I've got something for you. All I need is a hammer. I've brought a nail with me.'

'What? A hammer?'

'Yes, please. And then show me your room.'

'It's the pink room – the furthest bedroom at the back. I'll get a hammer.' She watched Matt carry the package carefully up the stairs. Then she went to the cupboard in the kitchen where Sita kept things like screwdrivers and pliers. She found a hammer and went up to join Matt, feeling weird. It wasn't easy being around people generally, but being around Matt was harder. She wanted to be the way she used to be, but she was different now. And it made it harder because he was so understanding. Of course she had told him about going back to No.42, and about the incident in the garden. He hadn't been shocked. Instead he'd said, 'Well, I'm no Angel!'

Jay knew he was referring to her obsession with *Tess*.

'And unlike him, I will always be there for you, Jay. Just one thing.'

'What?'

'Promise me you won't read *Tess* again – at least not for a few years?'

A smile tweaked the corner of her mouth. 'I promise.'

She watched him from the bedroom door as he started unwrapping the package. 'What is it?' She laid the hammer on the bed and sat down.

'It's a surprise,' he answered, 'and you're not to

look. So out you go.' He took her hands and pulled her off the bed, swooping in to kiss her before pushing her towards the door. 'And turn around until I say you can look.'

Jay leaned back against the wall and shut her eyes. She could hear him humming, and then hammering in the pink room, her room. She could hardly believe it. Matt was in her room, and maybe it wasn't so weird after all.

'OK, you can come and see now.'

He was grinning and pointing at the wall. Where there had been a space there now hung a mirror - her pink-heart mirror. She went closer. There was no crack in the glass. Matt had had it repaired. She put her hand up to it. Her fingers were trembling. Matt took her hand and held it tight, while she looked at her reflection. The girl she had last seen in the broken mirror looked different. She had been a stranger, beaten and broken, with shame stamped across her face.

This girl smiled back at her.

UK SUPPORT CENTRES

If you have been affected by any of the issues raised in this book, the following organizations can help you. These organizations can provide information and help, and direct you to services available in your area.

ASHA PROJECTS
www.ashaprojects.org.uk
UK Advice Line: 0208 696 0023
advice@asha.org.uk

CHILDLINE
www.childline.org.uk
UK Helpline: 0800 1111
(24 hours a day, 7 days a week)
Email and 1-2-1 online support available

KARMA NIRVANA
www.karmanirvana.org.uk
UK Helpline: 0800 5999 247
(Monday–Friday, 9am–5pm)
info@karmanirvana.org.uk

NSPCC
www.nspcc.org.uk
UK Helpline: 0808 800 5000
(24 hours a day, 7 days a week)
help@nspcc.org.uk

RAPE CRISIS
www.rapecrisis.org.uk
UK Helpline: 0808 802 9999
(every day 12-2.30 & 7-9.30pm)

About the Author

SAVITA KALHAN was born in India, but has lived in the UK most of her life. Savita graduated from Aberystwyth University with a degree in Politics and Philosophy. She was a Batik artist before getting married in the Philippines and going to live in the Middle East for several years, where she taught English and began to write.

Now living in North London, she spends her time writing, playing tennis, growing veg and super-hot chillies on her allotment, and loves to get the boxing gloves on.

Savita is a member of the Scattered Authors Society and blogs at An Awfully Big Blog Adventure. She runs a teen reading group at her local library in Finchley. Her debut novel, *The Long Weekend*, is a tense thriller about two boys who are abducted after school, and was shortlisted for the Fabulous Book Award.

You can visit Savita's website at www.savitakalhan.com.

Also available by Savita Kalhan

THE LONG WEEKEND

Kalhan builds tension expertly in this thriller. It is beautifully handled, without a trace of sentimentality, but with a credible and compassionate ending to a harrowing story – sadly, very much of our time.
Books for Keeps (5 Stars)

A tense contemporary thriller about two boys escaping from a remorseless abductor. Written plainly and directly, this is all the more cogent as it is a realistic scenario.
The Bookseller

The Long Weekend is a dark and powerful story full of menace and fear. Savita Kalhan has managed to get inside the mind of a terrified eleven-year-old boy and realistically write about his innermost feelings of fear, anger, self-pity, and deep hatred.
Mslexia

This book really is the definition of a page turner. I read it in one sitting.
Michelle Harrison

DISCOVER MORE STORIES

YOU'LL LOVE

AT

TROIKABOOKS.COM

#TROIKABOOKS

troika